CRIMSON POISON

SUSAN MOORE

nosy
crow

LOOK OUT
FOR

EMERALD SECRET

IT'S A RACE
TO UNLOCK
THE PAST

For Lilu. Dragons can be most useful.

First published in the UK in 2016 by Nosy Crow Ltd
The Crow's Nest, 10a Lant Street
London, SE1 1QR, UK

Nosy Crow and associated logos are trademarks and/or registered
trademarks of Nosy Crow Ltd

Text © Susan Moore, 2016
Cover © Alessandro "Talexi" Taini, 2016

The right of Susan Moore to be identified as the author of this work
has been asserted by her in accordance with the Copyright, Designs
and Patents Act 1988.

Printed and bound in the UK by Clays Ltd, St Ives Plc
Typeset by Tiger Media

Papers used by Nosy Crow are made from wood grown in
sustainable forests.

ISBN: 978 0 85763 449 8

www.nosycrow.com

FUTURE TECH AND OTHER COOL STUFF

FASTPAD: A flexible, tough, wafer-thin tablet computer, which can be rolled up. Invented by UK-based technology company Fenomenell.

GROOVERIDER: A low-slung, hydrogen-powered sports car with a distinctive grooved bonnet. Designed and manufactured by Choprider, Shanghai.

NEWSAMP: A 24/7 news service delivering ranked, hottest news stories.

OCTOZEB GOGGLES: Diamond-def, virtual-reality goggles designed and made by SPIN, Hong Kong.

OVERRIDER: A super-sized, six-wheeled all-terrain truck. Originally developed for the Chinese army by Choprider, Shanghai.

PICUP: A 3D photo-sharing chat zone, optimised for robot-uploads.

POPKO JUICE: A range of juice smoothies served in striped layers containing a secret Popko ingredient.

ROCKETBOAT: A hydrogen-powered, cigar-shaped speedboat, capable of rapid acceleration and speeds of up to 200mph.

SLAMBURGER: The ultimate Yanbian beefburger created by top Hong Kong chef Shen Slam. Shen's signature toppings are legendary, with Slamburger winning Best Hong Kong Burger (voted for by Big Dragon News) for the last five years.

SLIDER: A skateboard-shaped, electrically powered hover board with pop-up handlebars. The Slider was invented by Beijing Bikes' top engineer, Liu Lee, using the same principles of motion as the classic hovercraft from the twentieth century. Sales of Sliders have outstripped bicycles by four hundred per cent over the last two years.

SMARTSHEET: Wafer-thin, everlasting digital paper.

SMART T-SHIRT: An e-textile T-shirt containing soft, flexible screens on the front and back for display of movie clips, photos or text.

Chapter One
SCHOOL'S OUT

The dragon robot's green snout popped out of the top of Nat's blazer pocket as he scanned the racks of multicoloured Sliders with his amber eyes. There were so many yellow ones; Nat had no idea which one was hers.

"*Row ninety, rack eight*," Fizz said in his squeaky, digital voice.

A loud bell rang out across the lawn from the main building. The other classes would come pouring out at any moment and it would be end-of-term mayhem.

Nat reached into her backpack, pulled out her sky-blue helmet and jammed it on to her head. She couldn't wait to race out through the school gates. A whole month of holiday was waiting for her – no lessons, no early mornings. She could taste freedom on the warm afternoon breeze.

Lowering her tinted visor she ran down to row ninety at the far end of the shelter where her custom-made Slider sat in its rack. She touched her index finger to the back scanner. The rear lights lit up, the board lifted automatically off the rack, backed out and lowered through the air, coming to rest in hover mode at her side.

The silver handlebars whirred up out of the top of the board, locking into place. She threw her backpack over her shoulders and hopped up.

"*Incoming message from Central Post Office. You have a parcel awaiting customs inspection,*" said Fizz.

"Not now, Fizz," she said, reaching into her blazer pocket to pull him out. She set him down on the handlebars. His golden talons curled around the bar and he spread his emerald wings for a quick solar charge. The scales shimmered in the afternoon sun.

Loud voices and laughter erupted from behind. Nat turned to see that the other classes were out and stampeding in her direction. She caught sight of a flash of bright-red hair among them.

"Wings in, Fizz, before Henry spots us. *Zoula!*"

He snapped them back in. Nat pushed the handlebars forward and the Slider glided swiftly across the lawn. She waved at the security guard and passed through Weiwood School's tall iron gates.

CRIMSON POISON

"*Hai*, Nat," said Wen, scooting her orange Slider up alongside.

Wen had already taken off her school blazer and slipped on a short lime-green jacket. Nat pulled back on the handlebars to slow her pace. Wen's furry purple rabbit robot, Fu, turned her head from where she was clipped on to Wen's handlebars. Her rabbit eyes glowed bright blue when she spied Fizz, and she let out a high-pitched squeak. Fizz answered with a loud snort.

Wen laughed. "That voice upgrade you did makes him sound more like a pig than a dragon."

Nat shrugged her shoulders. "It was the closest I could get. No one knows what a real dragon sounds like anyway."

"True, oh wise one, but I'm guessing a roar would be more like it."

"We'd better get a move on. *Zoula!*" said Nat, pushing forward on her handlebars again.

Wen followed. Nat steered her board into a narrow designated Slider lane. They were in luck – it was empty. A rush of cool air brushed her cheeks as she picked up speed.

"Drop or Easy Rider?" she shouted, seeing the fork in the lane up ahead.

"Drop!" shouted Wen from behind.

"Hang on, Fizz!"

His talons lengthened at Nat's command, wrapping tighter around the handlebars. Nat leaned to the left, the board following her movement, which brought them to the crest of The Peak. For a moment she had a bird's-eye, panoramic view of Hong Kong's jungle of skyscrapers below, the thick blue ribbon of Victoria Harbour separating the island from the even taller, thicker tangle of Kowloon's mash-up of buildings. Cruise liners, ferries, junk boats, sloops, sea-going vessels of all shapes and sizes were carving white trails across the harbour waters.

She took the Pok Fu Lam turn. The sun-drenched vista vanished. Her Slider pitched off down a steep Slider-only lane carved through a dense forest of trees and bushes. She pushed the board's handlebars further forward and felt it accelerate, moving down the steep track at a fast clip. She zoomed past clumps of ferns and vines. The smell of damp earth and musty leaves hit her nostrils.

"*Zoinks!*" she cried, rounding a corner.

A huge tree had fallen across the Slider's path. Fizz's snout lit up bright red. Nat pulled back on the handlebars, bringing the Slider to an abrupt hover-only mode.

"*Ai yah!*" cried Wen, nearly crashing straight into the back of her. "I knew we should have taken Easy Rider."

Chapter Two
MAX-HOVER

"Maybe we can get over it," said Nat, sizing up the fallen tree.

"No chance," said Wen. "Our Sliders can't hover up that high. We'll have to turn around."

Nat moved the dial on her handlebars all the way up to Max-Hover setting. Fizz released a long plume of white smoke from his snout as the Slider lifted high up into the air.

"You're crazy!" shouted Wen.

Nat moved in slowly towards the tree, but the Slider only reached halfway up its side.

"Hold tight, Fizz," she said, hitting the Vertical Storage button.

The Slider flipped upright. Fizz started snorting. Nat hung on to the handlebars, her legs dangling down in the air.

"What are you doing?" said Wen.

Nat hit Max-Hover again. The Slider reset its ground level to where it was hanging in vertical-storage mode. It flipped back to horizontal and lifted higher up, above the tree trunk. Nat pushed the handlebars forward. She glided over it with ease.

"*Zoula!*" she called to Wen.

"*Ai yaaaaaaaah!*" came the reply.

Seconds later Fu's furry ears popped up over the trunk, followed by the top of Wen's orange helmet. Satisfied that her friend had made it, Nat pushed forward, zipping down Pok Fu Lam again at a fast clip.

Rounding a sharp bend she saw a flashing sky-scraper sign looming up ahead. The end of Fizz's snout started to flash red and he let out the deafening, ringing sound of an old-fashioned alarm clock.

"*Zoinks!* Fizz, you can cut the alarm now," she said, pulling back on the handlebars.

But he only stopped when the Slider speedometer hit the urban-zone limit of ten miles per hour.

Nat's Slider popped out of the trees on to Po Shan Road. Her hand flew up off the handlebars to block the glare of sunlight, which was reflecting off one of the glass skyscrapers further down the hill. Her Slider detected her move and automatically slowed to safety speed. She took the opportunity to glance over her shoulder. The nose of Wen's Slider was just coming out of the trees.

"Fizz, play Fu Jam," she said, accelerating down through the busy Mid-Levels district.

A cool bass guitar riff started to boom out of the speakers in her helmet, blocking out the din of the city. Then the music suddenly cut out, to be replaced by Fizz's deafening alarm again. She reined in the handlebars.

"You ruin all my fun," she said, slowing back down to the speed limit.

The music came on again for only a split second before Fizz cut in once more.

"*Call from Henry*," he announced.

She bit her lip as guilt momentarily swept over her.

"Take a message," she said.

Chapter Three
THE PACKAGE

The dog started to whimper and whine. A man in a grey uniform looked up from his FastPad to see the tip of a black tail wagging frantically over the top of the mountain of incoming parcels that they had to process before the end of the day.

He walked across the concrete floor of the inspection shed. He could hear the dog's claws furiously scrabbling against cardboard as it tried to dig something out.

"Hang on, Wokstar," he said, reaching into his pocket for a fresh pair of inspection gloves.

This was the time of year he dreaded – Christmas and Chinese New Year, a double-whammy of gifts being sent in to Hong Kong from every part of the world. Worse still, friends and family sent some very strange presents to their loved ones on the island. Last year he and Wokstar had discovered a sealed bucket of live piranhas, and a stuffed pet rat in a box wearing an astronaut suit.

Wokstar started to bark insistently. The man's heart began to beat faster. He pushed his way through a narrow gap in the mass of packages to find Wokstar's nose wedged in between two boxes. "Sit!" he commanded.

Wokstar did as she was told but her long black tail still thumped against a box. The man flicked on the pencil-thin torch, which hung around his neck beside his Hong Kong customs security card. Leaning down he cast the beam into the gap.

The sorting robot must have slipped up – they never processed such small items in the Oversized Parcel Inspection Shed. He reached down with both hands and pulled.

Out popped a jar-shaped package. Wokstar started to bark wildly, leaping up, trying to grab it from his hand.

"Down!" he shouted.

She obeyed. A tremor of excitement ran through his hand as he turned the package in the bright overhead light. His boring day had just got a whole lot more interesting.

Chapter Four
QUICK CHANGE

Nat turned into Cochrane Street. Rush-hour traffic had started early. Even the Slider lane was crawling along like a thousand-year-old tortoise. Gigantic super-buildings lined either side of the street. They were so close together that the blue sky above was reduced to a long narrow strip. Deep shadowy pockets of darkness hid between neon-lit rows of street-level shops and restaurants.

Nat rode along at a crawling pace past blacked-out Grooveriders transporting Hong Kong's elite. Less important officials sat in Overriders emblazoned with China's red sun. Striped electric buggies containing stressed-out office workers stood bumper to bumper with rumbling delivery trucks that were fuelled by wok fat.

"Cut Fu Jam, Fizz."

She needed to be alert for any crazy buggy drivers trying to do an illegal cut through the Slider lane. She was still sore from being knocked off by one two months ago.

As the music stopped she gritted her teeth. "Bun Jou", the most overplayed Cantonese rock song of the year, was blaring out of a local cosmetics shop. It was playing everywhere right now, and driving her crazy.

As she passed the Lucky Cat restaurant the smell of fried fish in garlic and ginger made her taste buds tingle. She slowed her Slider…

Suddenly a holographic boy with spiky hair appeared, blocking her path. He was floating in mid-air. She pulled back to hover-stop mode. Now she was twelve she was of legal age for holographic advertising and the novelty had still not worn off. As Virtual Posters went this was a top-notch one. She could see they'd used the latest RealCutis software to design and build it since the whole poster was in true 3D, using the light and shade of the current environment outside to tone the boy's appearance. It was pretty slick and must have cost a fortune.

"*Hai*, Nat, it's sale time at Trenko! Come on in and you'll receive a free gift with your purchase," announced the boy, holding up a neon-lit arrow, which pointed at the massive Trenko tower opposite.

"No, thanks," she said.

The boy waved, then vanished just as Wen whooshed

up next to her.

"*Ai yah!* Some old lady with worse eyesight than Granny Tang pulled out right in front of me. I had to swerve to miss her and then she drove her Slider like a slug," she said.

"*Your class at Ken's studio starts in five minutes,*" said Fizz.

Fu's eyes lit up bright purple and narrowed. Her nose twitched. She swivelled her head around.

"*Get to Ken's fast. You've got five,*" she squeaked at Wen, thumping her back paw on the Slider handlebar.

"Why do you give me such a hard time?" grumbled Wen.

"Because you're always late!" said Nat, laughing. "We'd better take the fast lane. *Zoula!*"

She turned off street level, along a ramp and on to the upper Slider lane, which ran above the Mid-Levels escalators.

Ken's jeet kune do studio on Lun Fat Street was located on the first floor above the Vegetarian Paradise restaurant, which had an all-you-can-eat special for thirty dollars. Nat and Wen pulled up outside and stacked their Sliders in the metered parking zone. Strips of dark-brown paint were peeling off the restaurant walls, leaving a sickly yellow colour that looked like an overripe banana oozing in the hot sun. They took off their helmets and ran up the narrow stairway.

A few boys were already warming up on the exercise mats that covered the floor in Ken's studio. A couple more were practising on the Mook Jong wooden dummies, which stood lined up against the back wall. Sun streamed in the long window, making the posters and photographs of Ken's kung fu hero, Bruce Lee, come to life.

Ken strode across the mats to meet them. He bowed his head and folded his arms across his chest.

They bowed their heads in unison. "*Sifu.*"

"Kung fu kittens would do well to be on time if they want to become tigers," he said.

"Sorry, the traffic was bad," said Nat.

"And our little fox is where?"

Nat shrugged, trying to ignore the stab of guilt. She really should have waited for Henry.

"Go and get ready," he said, turning back towards the class.

The girls' changing room was tiny. Ken had created it out of the old broom cupboard when Nat had joined his dojo. She was the first girl to join; Wen was the second – and last. Such was Ken's reputation that

most girls attended Kung Fu Babes, where Madame
Wu had a gentler way of teaching.

Nat unzipped her pack and removed her white
kung fu suit. She put Fizz to perch on the shelf next to
Fu. Side by side the two robots could not have looked
more different. Fu was one of the latest "Super-Cute,
Fresh and Furry" rabbit models from Soyto. Her
fur was electric purple, each individual hair fully
waterproof and self-cleaning. Her long silky ears
were lined with soft, blue, everlasting velvet, the
same colour as her eyes. She looked as if she'd just
been taken out of the box. Everything about her said
"cuddle me".

Fizz sat a head shorter than Fu. Nat could cradle
him in the palm of her hand. He was a one-off dragon
robot, designed and built by her father. Back then
he'd been ahead of his time, a piece of cutting-edge
technology. Now he was ancient. He couldn't do
any of the things that the newer, mass-produced
robots could do. He couldn't walk or jump. He
didn't have the nano-tech camera lens or the megamax
audio system, but he was her trusted friend with his
glittering mesh of feather-light scales, microchips,
nano-sensors and robotic limbs. His golden talons
were so strong that he could hang upside down like

a bat, and stay gripped on to a sail rope in a force ten gale (he'd had to do that a few times during typhoon season). At twelve years old, he was the exact same age to the day as Nat herself; he was definitely vintage.

"*Central Post Office package update – customs inspection in progress,*" he announced.

"Later, Fizz. That's not important right now."

Wen winced. "*Ai yah!* That pig voice does not work. You must be able to find something better. Why don't you look in the Soyto library?"

Nat pulled on her kung fu slippers.

"Soyto isn't compatible. Neither are most of the digital voice upgrades because he's so old. You're just going to have to get used to it. Oh no, what colour?" she said, looking back up and seeing a long black box in Wen's hand.

The corner of Wen's lips twitched up into a wicked smile. "Wait and see."

She pulled out a green comb. Looking in the small mirror that she'd glued to the back of the broom cupboard door a few months before, she started to run it through her spiky black hair. Each strand began to turn a bright purple with gold flecks.

Nat's eyes grew wide. "Only a fashionista like you would pick that," she said, laughing.

Wen giggled. "It's a retro nano-colour. Want to try it?"

Nat scrunched her long red hair up into a tight topknot. "No, thanks. You know I'm useless with all that stuff."

She stepped out of the broom cupboard just as her nine-year-old cousin came bursting in through the entrance door. His face was the same colour as his red hair, and he had a long bloody scrape down his arm.

"*Zoinks*, Henry!" she said. "Aunt Vera's not going to like that one bit."

Chapter Five
X-RAY

The customs officer set the package down on the polished steel bench and switched on the overhead light. He should have taken it next door to where the smaller packages were dealt with but his curiosity had got the better of him.

He put on his half-moon glasses and turned the jar-shaped parcel around under the light. Whatever was inside had been sewn into a well-worn brown leather pouch. It was like handling a relic from the past, the sort of thing you would find in a museum inside a glass case labelled something like *Tangut messenger pouch, circa 1290*. His hands began to shake; this was a proper piece of history, just like he'd seen in the virtual museums where he spent his evenings and weekends.

Whoever had sent it lived in Mongolia, judging by the postage marks. Scrawled in thick black ink below was an address:

CRIMSON POISON

J. Borjigin
PO Box 1288
Central Post Office
Hong Kong

Flipping it over, he ran his gloved hand across a seal of blue wax. Stamped into the wax was a howling wolf with its head thrown back. A trail of shapes streamed out of its mouth: a star, a half-moon and a triangle.

Holding it up to his nose he took a long sniff. More than anything, the smell reminded him of the musty old goats that his grandparents had kept on their farm up in Central China.

He picked up his FastPad and held it over the package.

"Level-five scan," he ordered.

The screen lit up bright blue.

"*Scan complete*," said the FastPad in its digital-readout voice. "*Negative dangerous, live or illegal elements found.*"

With that answer he knew he should now stamp the package "*Inspected by Customs*" and send it on its way. But instead of reaching for a clear customs bag off the shelf he picked up a knife.

He was about to slice through one of the thick gut

threads holding the parcel together when Wokstar started to bark. Blade poised, he looked over his shoulder as the far door opened and a tall woman appeared, striding across the floor in heavy boots.

"Get a move on!" she shouted, her voice booming across the shed. "Next lot of packages is about to be delivered."

He tried to hide the package behind his back but she was too swift.

"What's this doing here?" she said, grabbing it from the table.

"The robot sorter sent it," he replied.

She frowned. "You should have sent it over to my team."

He shrugged. "I thought I'd inspect it to save time."

"Save time?" she snorted. She waved her hand at the mountain of uninspected parcels. "You've got thirty minutes to sort this lot out otherwise I'll put you back on the night shift."

She swung round and stomped out, the mysterious, ancient package clasped in her hand.

Chapter Six
SCOWLER

"It's not Mummy who's hurt, it's me!" said Henry, tears pouring down his freckled cheeks. "If you'd brought me here and not Prissy then this would never have happened!"

Nat put her arm round his shoulders. She bit her lip as a wave of guilt washed over her.

"Prissy was cross because she had to drop me off and it was making her late to meet Candy so she tipped me off the back of her Slider on to the pavement. She drove off and just as I was getting up the chef came out of the restaurant and banged into me with his vegetable boxes. He didn't even say sorry. Ouch, it reeeeally hurts!"

Ken appeared and took hold of Henry's arm. He turned it one way, then the other, weighing up the damage. "It's superficial. You will live. Come with me. Nat, get the fashion queen out of the cupboard and start your warm-up."

Nat grabbed Wen. They stepped on to the mats and

began to stretch. Nat felt herself relax as she drew in deeper and deeper breaths.

"Hey," she whispered. "Let's do that mountain fight scene from *Heavenly Fires*."

Wen's eyes lit up. "OK. I'm Wanda, in her tangerine jumpsuit. It's so *ding*."

"*Ku!*" said Nat, and went to fetch a couple of bo-sticks off the rack at the side of the room. "You ready to wok and woll?"

They took position. Nat tossed a bo-stick to Wen. "Let's go from the steep cliff bit."

Nat raised her bo-stick and charged at Wen. Her friend blocked her. Nat tried again. Finally, with both hands on the stick, she locked and pushed Wen on to the mat, poised to knock her over the edge of the cliff just as Scowler had done. She raised her stick.

"Let's stop right there," said Ken, emerging from his office with a bandaged Henry in tow.

Nat froze. They set down the bo-sticks, bowed to each other and turned to their kung fu master.

"I have a feeling you two have been to the movies. Your moves are *gun fu*." Ken folded his arms across his black cotton jacket. Nat shrank from his piercing gaze. You never argued with Ken.

"Yes, *Sifu*. We were channelling *Heavenly Fires*."

CRIMSON POISON

"Ah yes, Scowler Stone and Wanda. Now, as Bruce Lee once said, 'Do not look for a successful personality and imitate it – be yourself.'" He paused for a moment. "You are both very talented and have skill, but you must use it honestly to express yourself, and not someone else."

"Yes, *Sifu*," they replied in unison, bowing their heads.

"Good, then let us work on what you are meant to be studying, Tiger Style. Today we will focus on Tiger Tail Kick. Spin to your right, go down on your left knee, place your hands on the ground for support then drive the bottom of your right foot backward at your opponent. Henry, you will sit, watch and learn."

It was a long session. Nat was sure Ken added on the extra twenty minutes as punishment. After more than a hundred Tiger Tail Kicks, her legs felt like lead as she headed for the broom cupboard.

The moment she stepped inside, Fizz's eyes flashed amber.

"*Central Post Office package update. Customs inspection clear. Parcel ready for collection. Total charge twenty-five dollars. Payable on—*" The message was cut off. "*Call from Jamuka,*" he announced from his perch on the shelf.

"Take it."

Fizz turned and spread his wings. There, on a three-inch, high-definition, flex-diamond-coated screen, was Jamuka in his kung fu gi, sitting cross-legged on the deck of the *Junko*. His grey hair was pulled back into a braid. Gobi, his green and white songbird, was sitting chirping away in her bamboo cage that was hanging off the boom of the central mast. The edges of the burnt-red sails that Ah Wong, their housekeeper, hadn't bothered to properly tuck in flapped in the wind. Behind him towered Hong Kong's skyline.

"I see you are still at Ken's," he said.

"He made us do loads extra and now I'm really starving."

"Then make haste back here. We are due at Uncle Fergal and Aunt Vera's in thirty minutes."

Her hand flew to her mouth – she'd completely forgotten. Any holiday feeling vanished in an instant.

"Do we have to?"

Jamuka leaned in closer to camera, peering over his half-moon glasses.

"I'll expect you back here in ten minutes. By the looks of you I imagine you will want to change before we leave."

Jamuka's voice was always soft – an iron fist in a

velvet glove. There was no point in trying to change his mind. He cut the call.

"*Wa sai!* Supper with the cousins on the last day of term? We'd better fuel you with a Popko juice before you go," said Wen.

Chapter Seven
BREATH

Nat took a long slurp through the spiral straw sticking out of her takeaway Popko cup. The taste of ice-cold strawberry and coconut was delicious. She pressed her tongue up to the roof of her mouth. The tiny bubbles, which were Popko's secret ingredient, exploded open, releasing a chocolate and caramel fizz. A smile spread across her face; there was no better taste in the world.

"*Driver approaching*," chirped NutNut, his tufted red squirrel ears robotically twitching up and out of Henry's backpack.

A navy-blue buggy with a gold teddy bear stamped on to its bonnet pulled up alongside the Popko booth where they were all standing. The driver hopped out wearing a matching suit and a big smile. He looked from the photo of Henry on his FastPad to where Henry was standing in his kung fu suit trying to quickly finish his Popko juice.

"Mr Walker, please step inside and I'll get you

fastened in," said the driver, opening the passenger door.

Henry groaned. "I can't wait to get a Slider next year. Then I'll never have to take a babyish buggy ride ever again."

Nat took his empty cup, lifted his backpack off the pavement and handed it to the driver.

"I'll see you shortly," she said.

"Tuck that arm in now, please," said the driver, ready to close the buggy door. "Looks like you had a nasty accident."

"He was kung fu fighting and his opponent's Claw move got him," said Wen with a wink at Henry.

"That was just before Henry finished him off with a Tiger Tail Kick," added Nat.

"*Ku!*" said the driver, obviously impressed.

Henry blushed and smiled.

"Thanks," he called out of the window, as the driver pulled out into the traffic.

"I'd better get a move on too," said Nat.

She hugged Wen goodbye, jumped on board her Slider and headed off towards the piers.

A few minutes later she came to a halt, hovering in a long static line of suited city workers on Sliders. It would take her a good twenty minutes just to get to the water at this rate. It was going to be quicker to walk.

She jumped off, lowered the handlebars and selected the Carry option on the digital-readout panel. The Slider flipped on its side, a small panel opened up and a long strap unfurled. Nat hooked it over her shoulder and stepped on to the pedestrian walkway. The hover mode kept the board lifted and light on the strap.

"Hey, watch it!" called a man, ducking her Slider as she turned into Man Yee Lane.

"*Zoinks*, sorry!" she said.

Groups of daytrippers from the mainland were crowded around a double row of stalls selling cheap robots, handbags and scarves, buying last-minute items before they had to leave. Nat had forgotten they'd be still there. She cut behind a row, where there was just enough room to dodge around the stalls' storage lockers.

"*Zao gao!*" she said, slipping and nearly losing her footing on some old vegetable slop.

By the time she made it out on to the waterfront she felt a familiar tightness wrapping across her chest.

"Fizz – air!" she said, tugging him out of her T-shirt pocket.

His eyes started to flash red.

"No alarm!" she said, beginning to wheeze.

She put his snout to her mouth. He fired two puffs of asthma medication, which swept down her throat into her lungs. Her airways relaxed, opening up. She let her hand drop and sucked in gulps of warm, salty sea air.

"What would I do without you?" she asked, lifting him up to her cheek.

He let out a long, low purr. It had been ages since she'd last had an asthma attack. She raised her head to the sky and wondered what could possibly have triggered it. The city's pollution levels were low right now, and she hadn't been going that fast...

Her eyes were drawn to the top of a sleek glass-and-steel rocket-shaped skyscraper towering above. SPIN, the world-famous computer games company, and her inheritance. Its gold double-helix sign was rotating on the tip of the rocket's nose.

A heart-wrenching longing for her parents bubbled to the surface. She tried to dismiss it as a result of the asthma attack, pushing it back down to where she'd buried it, deep inside, but the feeling wouldn't go away.

She slipped the Slider strap off her shoulder, lowered the board to the ground and sat down on it.

"Play family photo-reel two, Fizz," she said, cupping him in her hand.

She knew she shouldn't – she was already late – but seeing them there, alive on screen, was the only thing that made her feel whole again.

Chapter Eight
THE JUNKO

Nat pointed Fizz's snout towards the SPIN pier gate for security identification. The gate unlocked automatically and slid open. She loaded her Slider into the rack behind the gate.

Turning towards the water she saw a couple of brand-new high-spec Rocketboats moored up in the VIP area. She guessed they had come in for the weekly game-off competition at SPIN. She'd have been going herself if she didn't have to go out for supper.

Supper! She was late, very late, but she felt better for watching the photo-reel. She ran past the Rocketboats towards a massive ocean-going wooden junk that sat at the end of the pier, floating on the harbour's choppy waters. On top of each of the three masts, dragon and wolf-head flags fluttered in the breeze.

She could see Jamuka on deck, pacing. He was waving a hand around in the air, speaking to someone on his phone. She ducked down, hoping he wouldn't see her, and crept up to the junk's bow. Her eyes travelled along the boat's polished, planked hull. She was in luck: Ah Wong hadn't closed the porthole to her bedroom.

Jamuka's deep voice travelled down to where she was standing. He was talking to his trainer about Dragon Khan's form for tomorrow's race at Happy Valley. Good. Whenever he was discussing his racehorse he was one hundred per cent distracted from anything else going on.

Keeping close, she tiptoed along to where the brass-rimmed porthole stood open above her head. She plucked Fizz off her shoulder.

"I'm sending you in first," she whispered.

With a well-practised aim she tossed him up and through the window. A second later he let out two "all clear" squeaks. She was good to go.

Bending her knees she sprang upwards, making a grab for the porthole frame. She grasped on to it and pulled herself up and through. It was a tight squeeze but she managed to wriggle her way in. If she grew any more she'd have to find another secret way to sneak in.

She landed on her bunk next to Fizz and rolled on to the floor. Kicking off her boots she curled her toes into the soft sheepskin rug that covered the pale-grey floorboards. On the opposite side of her cabin the silver mural of a horse stretched the length of the wall. It glowed softly in the evening sun filtering through the porthole. Sunset was approaching fast. She must hurry.

Flinging open the door to her wardrobe, she scanned the shelves of neatly stacked Smart T-shirts, Slider shorts and sweatshirts. Her eyes moved over to the rail where a lone light-brown skirt hung on a solitary hanger. She frowned, took a deep breath and reached in for it. Next she pulled a pale-blue jumper off the top shelf.

Fizz let out a purr.

"No, Fizz, I do not look *ku*. I look like a dork, but I'm not going to let Aunt Vera have a moan about how I should stop dressing like a boy," she said, checking the finished outfit in the mirror.

The skirt was now way above the knee, and the sleeves of the jumper didn't quite reach her wrists. It would have to do. She grabbed her orange kung fu slippers from the drawer under her bed and lifted Fizz up on to her shoulder.

"*Zoula!*" she said, heading for the door.

Out in the narrow passageway she could hear Jamuka up on deck, still on the phone to his trainer.

She paused to check her hair in the small round mirror that hung in the middle of her mother's rogues' gallery. The paintings of weird and wonderful creatures always shocked anyone who hadn't seen them before. To Nat they were as familiar as old family portraits. Each one a headshot design, which her mother had painted in oil for SPIN's first virtual-world game. The Badgerbat was the most famous, with its furry blue-and-white-striped face framed by huge silver bat ears.

"Take this and hurry up. He's been waiting for you," said Ah Wong, appearing from the galley. She was wearing her flat white chef's hat and a big frown. Nat took the steaming bamboo basket from her.

"What's in it?"

"Steamed pork and onion dumplings. I made them an hour ago, per his orders, but they've been sitting waiting for your return."

"Sorry, I got delayed."

Ah Wong tut-tutted and returned to the galley, slamming the door behind her. Nat sighed. It was a good job she was old enough now not to have Ah Wong chaperoning her around town. Back then she had nicknamed her the Dark Shadow, as despite her attempts to escape her in the crowds Ah Wong always found her again. Now Ah Wong was relegated to the kitchen she was getting even grumpier.

Nat climbed up the ladder, out on to the deck. Gobi spied her from the cage and started to chirp loudly; Fizz let out a deafening squawk in reply. Jamuka turned from where he was standing on the hull's upper deck.

"I must go. I will see you on the track at eight," he said, finishing his call.

Instead of walking down the steps, he sprang like a cat on to the lower deck. He was so silent and quick that even after all the years of being her guardian he could still surprise her. She tried hard to second-guess him, but somehow he was always one step ahead of her.

"You are going to have to reprogram how Fizz responds to Gobi. That screeching will drive us all mad, Bao Bao."

"Will do. It's just that the upgrade I did needs fine-tuning. Is Dragon Khan ready to race?" she asked.

"Yes, the vet's given the all-clear, so we'll move round to Causeway Bay this evening. Ah Wong can sail round while we are at supper."

Nat made a mental note to tell Wen.

"*Central Post Office now closed. Pick-up of urgent parcel incomplete. Alert tomorrow?*" announced Fizz.

Jamuka raised an eyebrow. "Urgent parcel not picked up?"

"Ah, yes. It's addressed to you. I'll get it in the morning," said Nat.

"When I gave you the duty of managing our post box I put my trust in you to make collections on a timely basis."

Nat shrugged. "It's only a parcel. Besides, they want twenty-five dollars for it because customs inspected it. I will pick it up in the morning, I promise. Now, do we *really* have to go to Aunt Vera and Uncle Fergal's?"

Jamuka put his hand on her arm, guiding her towards the gangplank.

"Aunt Vera does not entertain excuses, unlike myself."

Chapter Nine
WETLEY TOWERS

Jamuka drove the sleek Grooverider with its blacked-out windows silently through the streets of Central to the Mid-Levels. Wetley Towers was once the newest and tallest building on Robinson Road but now it was surrounded on all sides by even taller skyscrapers, which blocked its once magnificent views.

He swung in through the iron gates and drove up to the marble steps in front. The car door lifted up like a gull's wing and Nat climbed out, self-consciously adjusting the hem of her skirt. She'd rather be anywhere but here right now.

The doorman took the car. Nat and Jamuka walked up the steps and into the lobby, which housed the largest crystal chandelier in Hong Kong. Its glass crystals dripped like icicles. Nat had the same thought every time. Any moment now it would come crashing down on top of them and shatter into a million pieces. She grabbed Jamuka's hand, yanking him towards the lift.

"Oh, Nat, you look deeeevine!" screeched Aunt Vera, opening the door to apartment number 1187.

Her long red talons gripped Nat's shoulders as she pecked her on each cheek. A thick, oily cloud of Super Spice perfume made Nat choke. Over her aunt's platinum helmet of hair, Nat caught sight of Henry's older sister, Prissy, who had a mean scowl on her face.

"Good evening, Vera. Our apologies for being late," said Jamuka with a short bow.

He presented her with the bamboo basket of dumplings. Aunt Vera gave him a curt nod, took the basket and without a second glance dumped it on the hall table. She steered Nat by the arm through to the sitting room.

"Tiki Bar is open, Jamuka. I want to hear your racing tips!" called out Uncle Fergal, her father's half-brother.

He was standing in the corner of the room, behind a wooden bar that was loaded with bottles in every shape, size and colour. His meaty fingers were combing the last remaining strands of hair over his bald head.

"A lychee fizz would be most welcome," said Jamuka, heading for a drink.

Quick as a flash, Prissy opened her hand to reveal

her glitter cat robot sitting in her palm. Its eyes started to blink as Prissy snapped photos.

"A photo of Nat looking like a girl! What a good idea," said Aunt Vera.

"I hate having my photo taken," Nat protested in vain.

Aunt Vera held up her hand. "Nonsense. These are special moments in your growing up, Natalie, and must be recorded."

"I can't wait for everyone to see you on my Picup," whispered Prissy. "You look so lame."

Prissy was a fashion victim. Her pink mini-dress had a letter "S" in gold across the front for the designer Shan-xi (Nat referred to him as Fancy Schmancy), who had a shop that ran across an entire block downtown. Prissy's hair was fluffed up and pinned to one side with a plumage of canary-yellow feathers. The pink mules on her feet each had a matching diamanté "S" on the heel.

Nat contemplated unleashing a swift kung fu move but she knew Jamuka would punish her. Instead, she bit her tongue at the prospect of becoming a laughing stock among Prissy's friends.

"*Hai*, Nat," said Henry, walking in.

His arm was freshly bandaged from shoulder to

wrist like an Egyptian mummy.

"What happened, Henry?" called Jamuka from his position at the bar.

"A nasty chef bumped into my darling boy with a metal box," said Aunt Vera, ruffling Henry's hair. "He's been so brave about it."

"Didn't you tell her about Prissy dumping you off her Slider?" Nat whispered in Henry's ear.

He shook his head. "Prissy said she'd never give me a lift on her Slider ever again if I did."

Nat shot Prissy a withering look but it was met with a sly smile.

"I've downloaded the new *Rainskid* game. Want to check it out?" said Henry, holding up NutNut.

Nat glanced over at the Tiki Bar. Uncle Fergal and Jamuka were now in deep conversation, heads bent over a FastPad, which no doubt had the racing report loaded. Prissy had moved on to the sofa and was occupied with her glitter cat robot, and Aunt Vera had disappeared, most likely to boss around her maid, Ming, in the kitchen. Her little cousin was easily her best bet for entertainment.

"*Ku!* Let's do it," she said.

Chapter Ten
REAL FAMILY

When Aunt Vera announced that supper was being served, Nat's stomach lurched. She remembered how delighted Prissy had been to share her mother's notebook with Nat, when the cousins had been left alone in the apartment a few weeks earlier. It contained a collection of Aunt Vera's recipes filed in three groups: recipes for A-list, B-list and C-list guests. At the back of the book were lists of guests. With a wicked smile, Prissy had pointed out that both Nat and Jamuka had a "C" marked next to their names.

As well as the prospect of a terrible meal, Nat also loathed where they had to eat it – in the aquamarine dining room. Everything in it was Aunt Vera's favourite colour. The walls, ceiling, floor, table, chairs, place settings – even the glasses matched. And to top it all Aunt Vera was wearing an aquamarine dress this evening. When she took her seat she blended in so perfectly that her head seemed to float in mid-air.

Across the table from Nat sat Prissy. Her scowl had

been replaced by another sly look of satisfaction. Her glitter cat trotted over to Nat. When it reached her, the side of its body turned into a small screen. Prissy had animated the photo of Nat so that she appeared to be dancing. Worse still, she had replaced Nat's legs with pig's trotters. There was a note underneath from one of Prissy's inner circle of vile friends: *LOL, wot a loser. Oink! Oink!*

Nat felt tears of humiliation welling up. She wished she had never worn the stupid skirt, and she loathed her cousin. She balled her hands into fists and glared across the table as the cat flicked its tail and trotted back to Prissy. She wished she could send Fizz over with a suitably poisonous message, but he hadn't been upgraded to walk or flick his tail. Sometimes she hated having such an old model.

"Loser," Prissy mouthed.

Ming entered carrying a large steaming silver bowl, which she set down in the centre of the table. Nat peeked over the edge to find a pool of tomato sauce. Noodles and yellow chunks of tinned pineapple bobbed on its surface. Hawaiian Tropical Sardine Delight – again.

"Grub's up," said Uncle Fergal, rubbing his belly.

Nat picked up a noodle with her chopsticks, closed

her eyes and swallowed. It tasted like a sweet, slimy worm.

The discussion turned to what was happening in Uncle Fergal's banking world. She wondered if this was what normal families talked about around the meal table. In *Flapjack Family*, her favourite American TV show, they always seemed to be having a great time with lots of jokes and laughter. She wondered if that was how her mother's childhood had been in San Francisco. Here in Hong Kong, though, it was a very different story. Supper at Wetley Towers was one big fun-sponge, soaking up joy in seconds.

When Ming brought in bowls of lychee jelly topped with tinned, long-life cream, Jamuka excused himself to make an important call.

"With the school holidays underway, we should take this opportunity for you to get more involved with your real family," said Aunt Vera, turning her attention to Nat. "I think it's high time you came to stay with us for a while."

Nat gulped. She had never stayed with them, and she never planned to.

"What?" said Prissy in horror.

"*Ku!*" grinned Henry.

"Jamuka is my real family too," said Nat.

Aunt Vera's pursed lips stretched into a thin smile. She reached over, laying her bony hand over Nat's. When Nat tried to slip hers out from underneath, her aunt tightened her grasp.

"He's your guardian, yes, but he's not blood, is he?"

Nat dropped her spoon.

"Come on, Vera, that's a bit strong, isn't it?" said Uncle Fergal.

Aunt Vera held up her hand to silence him.

"Fergal," she snapped. "Nat's of an age now where she needs female guidance, and it should come from her proper family."

"No, I don't," said Nat.

Aunt Vera leaned in close to her ear.

"You're fast becoming a young woman and I can help you make the most of yourself. As heiress to such a large fortune, you need to be groomed before you enter society."

Nat swallowed. "I'm fine as I am."

Sensing Nat's growing alarm, Fizz's eyes started to flash red. Nat glanced at the doorway. Where was Jamuka when she needed him?

"And we're off to Sanmen Island," she continued. "So I couldn't come and stay anyway."

Aunt Vera's eyes narrowed. She loosened her grip.

CRIMSON POISON

"Oh, I hadn't been told," she sniffed.

"Yes," Nat added quickly. "We're leaving the day after tomorrow, after the race at Happy Valley."

"Well, we'll have to do it when you return then. It's important that we have some girls' time together," she said with a hideous smile.

Nat shuddered. Whatever Aunt Vera had in mind, it was bound to be torture.

Chapter Eleven
THE OLD WOMAN

Later that night Nat was back in the safety of her cabin on the *Junko*. She crossed the rug to a gold-lacquered chest that had belonged to her mother. Lifting the lid she carefully removed a faded lemon-yellow kimono. She buried her face in the soft silk and inhaled the faint smell of roses.

The years fell away. She was transported back into the safety of her mother's arms. If only she was still alive, if only she was there to offer female guidance, then Aunt Vera wouldn't be sniffing around.

She unfolded the kimono and wrapped it around her. Crawling into bed she waited for sleep to come, cocooned in the memory of her mother. Only a few fleeting memories remained though – her mother's beautiful smile, her laughter and her gentle touch.

"Fizz, play sailing movie five," she said.

Beside her on the pillow Fizz opened his wings. Instantly Nat's ears were filled with the sound of ocean waves. A young woman with long blonde hair flying across her face in the breeze grinned into the camera. Behind lay a clear blue sky over a white-capped sea. She was bouncing a baby in her arms, who squealed in delight.

"And how is Mrs Walker today?" came a man's voice, off camera.

"Great!" said the woman. "As is our gorgeous girl." She lifted the baby up higher.

"One, two, three, four, five, once I caught a fish alive," she sang in her soft Californian accent.

The baby giggled.

"Wait, I'm coming in," said the man. "Just let me perch Fizz on the wheel."

Nat smiled at her dad's thick Scottish accent. The camera pulled back to reveal the deck of the *Junko*. He walked into shot wearing a white T-shirt and blue shorts. His black wraparound sunglasses were propped up on his thick dark hair. He walked over and scooped up the baby, lifting her even higher.

Nat put her hand to the screen, her fingers tracing her mother's face, then her father's, and finally her own. Her parents looked so young and happy. She watched as her mother launched a kite up into the wind while her father held her, pointing up to where it bobbed and weaved. If only she could climb into the screen…

Her eyelids grew heavy. She blinked to try and keep them open but sleep called…

And the nightmare began.

She was standing in a clearing in the middle of a forest, barefoot on the snow-covered ground. Giant fir trees formed a wall around her. All around was silent and still. Looking down, she saw that she was wearing her purple kung fu outfit. The cold was intense, turning her body into a block of ice. Suddenly an ear-piercing scream tore through the air as a crow-like woman in a black cloak flew out from the trees. Nat thought she looked about a hundred years old with her long white hair and leathery brown skin.

Panic rose in Nat's throat. She tried to move into a kung fu crouch, ready to do battle, but she was frozen to the spot. As the woman drew closer, brightly patterned red petals began to rain from the sky. The old woman opened her mouth and reached towards Nat with her wrinkled hands. Nat screamed.

Chapter Twelve
RED PETALS

Nat woke up on the floor, tangled in her sheet.

Fizz was lying at her side, the sailing movie still playing on the screen in a continuous loop.

"Fizz, stop movie," she said.

He folded in his wings.

"Time?"

"Three twenty a.m."

She groaned, turned on to her side and unravelled herself. Her head was spinning. Maybe it was the revenge of the Hawaiian Tropical Sardine Delight. Getting slowly to her feet she fastened the kimono's belt.

"Let's head up," she said, picking up Fizz.

She climbed to the upper deck and sat down in one of the blue deckchairs. Ah Wong had moored the *Junko* close to the Royal Hong Kong Yacht Club. The mast on top of the white circular clubhouse was twinkling with Christmas lights. Behind it, Causeway Bay's skyscrapers huddled together, their bright lights set against an inky-black night sky. Behind them, unseen, lay Happy Valley racecourse, and there in the cemetery right above it lay her parents.

Nat closed her eyes, wishing for the millionth time that things were different – that she wasn't an orphan and her parents were still alive. She loved Jamuka. He was her rock, her protector and sole guardian. He'd been appointed according to her parents' wishes and was the only person they had really trusted. But he still couldn't fill the black hole left by their absence. And now Aunt Vera was trying to step in…

A cloud passed over the moon, accompanied by a cold gust of air that rattled through the *Junko*'s rigging above. Nat hunkered down in the deckchair and stroked Fizz's scaled head. His eyes started to glow bright purple.

"What would I do without you?" she whispered.

A pot clattered to the floor in the galley below, making her jump. She peered over the side. Light shone through the porthole. Either Jamuka or Ah Wong was up.

"You should be in bed, Bao Bao," said Jamuka as Nat walked into the kitchen. "It's the middle of the night."

"I had a nightmare," she said, sitting up on one of

the stools at the marble-topped counter.

Jamuka was spooning ground coffee into his old-fashioned stovetop espresso pot. She spotted the coffee tin and wrinkled her nose.

"*Zoinks!* Not the Vietnamese weasel coffee."

He smiled and held the open tin out towards her. She recoiled, nearly falling off her stool.

"It helps me think."

"Don't you want to sleep?"

"Not tonight. I must send good thoughts to Dragon Khan."

"Can you send some to Aunt Vera too, and stop her bothering me?"

"Was that what your nightmare was about?"

Jamuka screwed the top on to the espresso pot and twisted the gas knob on the stove. A blue flame shot out, heating the water.

"No. There was an old woman, like a crow, and red petals. It was raining red petals."

Jamuka looked up from the tin, his eyes widened in surprise.

"What's the matter?" she asked.

His brow creased. He shook his head.

"It's nothing. You just prompted an old memory, that's all. Hot chocolate?"

She nodded.

"Do not concern yourself with Aunt Vera. I will deal with her when we are back from our trip to Sanmen. What are your plans tomorrow? I have to be up at the stables by eight."

Nat picked out a plum from the fruit bowl that hung from the ceiling.

"I've promised to take Henry to SPIN to try out the new Octozeb goggles."

"Good. Now, since I sense that neither of us is tired, and there won't be time for practice in the morning, let us fuel ourselves with our drinks and head to the dojo."

Nat chugged her hot chocolate, headed down to her cabin and pulled her purple kung fu suit off its peg. Her hand rested for a moment on her black sash – out of her reach until she had mastered the Five Animal Style.

"One day," she said, taking the brown sash instead.

She scrunched her hair up into a topknot and ran out of her cabin to the end of the passageway where a rope ladder led down to the dojo studio.

It was still dark outside, but inside the studio was bathed in soft overhead night-lights. Jamuka was waiting, standing in the middle of the wooden floor, his hands in prayer position. The door slid shut behind her, closing off the square room with paper screens. Nat took her place opposite him.

"Empty your mind," he said, bowing his head.

She closed her eyes but the old woman's face instantly appeared. The more she tried to block it out of her mind's eye, the more vivid it became.

"Warm up," he said.

She automatically lifted her arms to hold an imaginary ball, moving through a series of t'ai chi moves, which were as familiar to her as her own breathing, but she couldn't empty her mind of the old woman's face.

"Position," he said.

She planted her feet hip-width apart. Jamuka gave a faint nod.

With a left arm punch she aimed at his left shoulder, but he swiftly blocked its path with his forearm. She swivelled from the waist, throwing her right leg up into a high kick. Jamuka blocked her again. She threw another punch, this time with her right arm then the left in quick succession but he blocked her each time.

Thinking she would surprise him, she sprang up into a double-leg kick position but instead of seeing Jamuka's head in her path her vision was blocked by a storm of red petals.

She landed hard on the mat. Jamuka's hand slid under her armpit, helping her up.

"Is something wrong, Bao Bao?" he asked.

She blinked. The petals were gone.

"Red petals. That was all I could see. Red petals."

Chapter Thirteen
CENTRAL POST OFFICE

Nat turned her Slider into the South Fin entrance of the SPIN rocket skyscraper. She passed through the shimmering silver air curtain and entered a sky-soaring glass atrium.

Glancing up she saw that the café and shopping level above were already teeming with customers. She pulled into the parking zone and found a free slot.

"*Reminder. Parcel from Central Post Office awaiting collection,*" announced Fizz.

"After the gaming session," said Nat.

A robotic Badgerbat swooped down, coming to a hover in mid-air.

"*Welcome to SPIN. Can I help you?*"

Nat held up Fizz.

"Identify," she said.

Fizz's eyes lit up as he swapped data with the Badgerbat.

"*Welcome, Rainfox. Your gaming session is due to start in ten minutes in Six Alpha,*" said the Badgerbat.

"Thanks," she said, enjoying the anonymity of her gaming handle.

No one knew who she really was, except a few SPIN employees. If they did she'd be mobbed. Instead she had always been known as Rainfox, the name her father had registered for her when she was born.

"*Call from Henry*," announced Fizz, retracting his talons from the handlebar.

She picked him up. His wings spread and Henry appeared, filling the screen with his round, freckled face. He was wearing his black Slider helmet.

"*Hai*, Henry."

"I'm still at Wetley Towers. Prissy's giving me a lift but she's freaking out about her hair," he whined.

Off screen she heard Prissy let out a screech.

"Don't tell her that, you little snitch!"

Henry leaned into camera. "She borrowed Mummy's new hair curlers but it's made her hair all fried and frizzy," he whispered. "Please will you come and get me?"

Nat had a sudden brainwave.

"No, I've got a better idea. Get Prissy to drop you at Central Post Office and I'll meet you there in twenty minutes."

She cut the call.

"Fizz, tell the Badgerbat to rebook our gaming session for ten o'clock."

Fizz's eyes flashed red. Nat turned her Slider around and headed out into Central.

Nat heard Prissy's approach before she saw her. The boppy beat of The Frou-Bunnies girl band came blasting up the post office ramp. Seconds later a hot-pink Slider with glitter finish appeared, its rider in a matching helmet, wearing a pair of Shan-xi yellow hotpants with matching jacket. Sitting on the back of the board, strapped into the extender seat was Henry, red-faced with embarrassment.

"He's all yours," said Prissy, pulling up to a hover.

She looked Nat up and down, her eyes narrowing with disdain as she took in her blue Slider shorts, boots and Smart T-shirt.

"I see what Mum means. You do look like a boy," she sneered, releasing Henry's seat straps. Kicking her foot back she booted Henry off the Slider.

"Ouch!" he cried.

Prissy thrust forward her handlebars. Her Slider lurched forward and off.

"Losers!" she shouted back over her shoulder.

"I wish I could trade her in for another sister,"

moaned Henry as she disappeared down the ramp.

Nat put her hand on his shoulder and steered him towards the glass doors.

"Don't worry about her. Let's grab the package I've got to pick up and head over to SPIN."

"*Ku* dragon," said the woman behind the counter, when Nat pointed his snout at the post office check-in screen.

"Thanks."

The woman smiled.

"I've never seen a robot like him before. They're all so big these days."

"He's vintage. Pay fee, Fizz."

Fizz's eyes lit up bright green as he communicated with the screen. Seconds later a hatch in the wall slid open and a metal robotic arm swung out, depositing the parcel on the counter. It was sealed inside a clear plastic customs inspection bag.

"Ah, you're the one this is for," said the woman. "Looks like it should have been delivered a couple of centuries ago. Ha ha!"

"*Zoinks*," said Nat, taking it from her.

She peeled off the "*Inspected by Customs*" tape and reached inside the bag.

"Wow, looks like it came from a museum!" said Henry.

Nat gasped at the jar-shaped, leather-bound package. Henry let out a low whistle.

"*Ku!* Let's open it."

"No, it's for Jamuka," she said, seeing the address. "Fizz. Call him."

Fizz beeped, his eyes flashed amber and he spread his wings. Jamuka appeared on screen wearing round mirrored sunglasses. He was down on the racetrack holding the reins of an enormous chestnut horse.

"Dragon Khan looks well," said Nat, noticing his glossy coat.

"The vet has declared him back on top form. I see you have finally made it to the post office."

"It's for you."

She held the package up to the screen. Jamuka whipped off his sunglasses. His face turned ashen.

"What?" said Nat, looking back down at the parcel.

There was a pause before he spoke. When he did he sounded hoarse, as if the breath had been sucked out of him.

"Bring it here as fast as you can, Bao Bao."

"What's the matter? What's in it?" she said.

Jamuka levelled his gaze at her. Nat detected

something she had never seen in his eyes before. Fear. Her heart started to thump.

"Just get here as soon as you can."

"You want us to come to Happy Valley?"

"Yes."

"But—"

Before she could finish, he cut the call. Fizz beeped, folding in his wings.

"Do you think it's a bomb?" asked Henry.

Nat felt a pang of guilt. If only she'd picked it up yesterday.

"Don't think so. I've never seen him look like that before. *Zoula!*"

She turned and headed back towards the lifts.

Henry frowned. "But what about our trip to SPIN?"

Chapter Fourteen
HAPPY VALLEY

Nat turned her Slider into the Happy Valley owners' entrance and pulled up to a hover at the gate. A racetrack security guard dressed in a green jacket walked out of his booth.

"Natalie Walker to see Jamuka Borjigin," she said.

He looked from her to Henry, who was sitting in the extender seat at the back.

"With Henry Walker," she added.

He nodded, peeled a numbered red sticker off the sheet and stuck it on to her handlebars.

"You're expected at the Pat Carey stable. Don't stop off anywhere else. You're not really meant to be here," he said.

The barrier started to lift. Nat looked up ahead. There were three separate lanes. She'd never been allowed in before.

"Which one do I take?"

He pointed to the one on the far left. "Level Seven. They're expecting you."

She pushed the handlebars forward and the Slider moved off. A little way along she turned a sweeping corner to find a tall, round white building looming up ahead. She drove up the ramp and inside. The lane split. Ahead stood a set of gates with a black and white sign above saying, *"Level One. Delioto Stables"*.

She continued along the right fork. It started to twist up and up like a helter-skelter.

"They keep horses in here?" said Henry through the headset in her helmet.

"Yes, it's the new stables," said Nat.

"It's like Wetley Towers," said Henry. "But for horses. It'd be *ku* to live here."

By the time they reached Level Seven Nat felt dizzy from the climb. She pulled up at the gates and pressed a red buzzer. Moments later a thin man in rubber boots appeared.

"Hey, what are you kids doing here? You've got to be eighteen," he said in a gruff voice.

"We're here to see Jamuka Borjigin. It's urgent," said Nat.

Someone shouted from behind the gate. Nat couldn't quite hear what they said but the thin man disappeared back inside and the gates swung open. The smell of sweet hay and warm horses hit Nat's nostrils as she pulled in. She wrinkled her nose.

"Park here," said the thin man, pointing to a spot between two Sliders emblazoned with yellow and black stripes, and the words *"Pat Carey Racing"*.

"I feel sick," said Henry, removing his safety strap and jumping to the ground.

"Follow me," said the man, ignoring him.

Nat put Fizz on her shoulder, grabbed Henry by the arm and set off after him. They passed through a set of metal doors into the stables. It was a tall, open space with huge paddle fans attached to the ceiling, which were rotating slowly, creating a cool downward breeze. A central corridor ran the length of the floor. On either side stood a row of loose boxes. The wooden lower doors were all locked with digital key codes. The railings above were painted in black and yellow stripes, making it feel like a giant beehive. A few horses had their heads stuck out over the doors.

A grey horse whinnied as they walked past. Nat was so used to robotic animals that she jumped in surprise.

Halfway down the row, the thin man disappeared off to the right.

"This way!" he called.

Nat broke into a run, anxious not to lose him.

"Hey, wait for me!" said Henry, trailing after.

She found a narrow alleyway, wide enough for a horse to pass through. It opened out on to an open-air exercise yard, high above ground level. Jamuka stood talking to a white-haired man wearing a black polo shirt and jodhpurs. They were watching Dragon Khan being walked around on a long rein by a stable hand.

"Swift like a bird, not slow like a tortoise, Bao Bao," said Jamuka, seeing her.

"We came as fast as we could," said Nat.

"Natalie Walker, Henry Walker, this is Pat Carey," said Jamuka.

The white-haired man smiled and nodded towards them.

"A pleasure to meet you both," he said in a thick Irish accent.

They shook hands. Nat reached into her backpack and pulled out the package.

"Here," she said, handing it over.

Jamuka's hand shook as he took it from her.

"Can I have the stamps for my collection?" asked Henry.

"Not now, Henry. Please stay with Mr Carey. Bao Bao, come with me."

CRIMSON POISON

He led her to a shaded viewing area.

"Take a seat," he said, sitting down on one of the folding chairs.

"What's in it?" she asked, watching him carefully turn the package over in his long fingers.

There was a soft cracking sound as he broke the blue wax seal on the base. He pulled the leather packaging off to reveal a silver jar stamped with star shapes. He unscrewed the lid and extracted a piece of damp grey cloth. His fingers trembled as he peeled it open. Inside lay a large red petal. It was divided into two shades of red – one very dark, almost black; the other bright scarlet – by a jagged electric-blue line. On the inside of the cloth, bold words had been written in black ink. Jamuka narrowed his eyes, scanning them. His brow furrowed with deep lines. He took a sharp intake of breath, slipped off the chair and fell to his knees.

Chapter Fifteen
ROCKETBOAT

Nat dodged in and out of the busy Slider lane traffic trying to beat Jamuka back to Causeway Bay. With Henry in the extender seat she had to be careful not to whip round anyone too quickly, otherwise the back would fishtail out.

"I'm feeling sick again," moaned Henry.

She eased off the throttle.

"At this rate, he'll be gone," she grumbled. "Fizz, give me Jamuka's location."

Fizz raised his snout up off his chest from where he was hunkered down over the handlebars. His eyes flashed as he checked in with Jamuka's FastPad.

"*On board the* Junko," he announced.

She gritted her teeth. "Henry, sorry, but hang on tight."

"What?" he cried, as she turned the Slider out of the congested Slider lane and into the flow of road traffic.

Fizz's eyes flashed red, a spurt of smoke pluming out of his snout.

"*Illegal move!*" he blasted out.

"I know," said Nat. "But it's the only way to get there in time."

She slotted in behind a wok-fat-fuelled delivery truck and a city buggy, which were clipping along down Canal Road. The buggy driver beeped his horn but Nat took no notice.

"What if Mummy finds out?" shouted Henry, hanging on at the back.

"She'll never know," said Nat, pushing the Slider up to top speed.

She'd rather lose her licence than not see Jamuka before he left. She still had no idea why he had to leave immediately. All she knew was that the package contained some very bad news about his Clan in Mongolia. He'd run out of the stables, leapt into his Grooverider and taken off at top speed, heading towards the *Junko*. A chill ran through her as she thought of the red petal again. It was exactly the same as the ones that had rained down in her nightmare.

"*Police ahead*," announced Fizz, the tip of his snout flashing red.

Nat tucked in behind the truck. Seconds later they passed a stationary black patrol car marked with a red sun on its doors. A policewoman had pulled over a city buggy.

"Phew!" said Nat.

"We could have been locked up in jail," moaned Henry.

Nat took the Royal Yacht Club turning and opted to take a short cut over the lawn towards the tall masts of the *Junko*, which were peeping over a line of super-yachts.

BOOM! The Noon Day Gun blasted out across the bay. Henry yelped.

"*Zoinks*, Henry! You know they do that every day," she said, laughing.

"I'd forgotten and don't laugh at me. It's not funny."

"Sorry."

She whisked them up the *Junko*'s gangplank, flipped off the power switch and jumped down off the Slider, leaving Henry strapped in as it lowered on to the *Junko*'s deck.

"Hey, wait for me!" he shouted.

Nat leapt in through the central hatch, landing in the passageway. She ran past her cabin until she reached the last door at the end.

Jamuka was inside, packing the few items laid out on his bed into a Kevlar backpack. She leapt on to the mattress.

"Please let me come with you! I know it'll be a hard journey but I'm a fast runner and one day I'll be a black belt if I practise hard enough…"

Jamuka stopped. He sat down next to her, taking her hand in his. "You are the most important person in the world to me. But my Clan is in danger so it is my duty to go to them."

"What danger?"

"A strange and terrible sickness has fallen upon the Clan and the wolf pack. The elders say that the Mana speaks of danger from outside and devastation within," he whispered.

"Mana?" said Nat.

She quietly tapped Fizz's head. He squeaked and popped up out of her top jacket pocket. His eyes lit up and his ears twisted round to listen and record. Her mind was racing through the stories that Jamuka had told her of his Clan in Mongolia. They lived high up on the Steppe in a land of endless forests and grassy plains.

Her bedtime stories had been filled with tales of his childhood: riding horses faster than the wind, hunting with wolves in the dark of night, swimming in ice-cold rivers. They were fairytales, a world away from Hong Kong. Now it seemed that the ancient-looking package was bringing them to life.

"When there is a problem to solve, the Clan elders climb to a mountaintop at sunset and wait for the moon to appear. From there, they watch the land below, looking for the slightest changes in nature. These changes produce strange flickers of light called Mana from which the elders can predict the future. They say the Mana has called for me."

"But why you? Can't they just get a doctor?"

Jamuka picked up a small tin of Vietnamese weasel coffee and loaded it into the backpack. He took a deep breath and exhaled loudly. "There is more to this than what a doctor can prescribe."

Out of the corner of her eye Nat spied a squirrel's head peering around the cabin doorway. Its eyes were lit up, electric blue, and its ears were pricked, which meant only one thing.

She ran out to find Henry on his knees holding NutNut, who was filming what was going on inside.

Seizing NutNut from Henry, she pressed its black shiny nose. The robot's eyes snapped shut, its ears flattened against its head.

"This is private!" she said.

"What's Mana again?" he asked.

She pointed up the passageway.

"Go up on deck. I'll be up soon."

He scowled and stomped off.

"I want to come with you," she said, turning back to Jamuka.

He picked the star jar up off the bed and handed it to her.

"Look after this while I am gone."

The weight of the jar felt as if it was anchoring her to the boat, stopping her from leaving with him.

"How do I get in touch with you? You told me there's no reception where the Clan is."

"Just use Fizz to leave me messages and I will find a way to check them."

He zipped up his backpack and slung it over his shoulder.

"What will I do without you?"

She swallowed hard. Jamuka had never left her, not once, since her parents had died.

"Ah Wong will care for you until my return."

The loud roar of a Rocketboat engine came blasting in through the porthole.

"We'd better go up. That's my ride to the airport," he said, heading out into the passageway. Out in the bay a silver torpedo-shaped vessel sat menacingly on the water, its engines rumbling. Henry was leaning over the side, holding NutNut.

"*Ku* Rocketboat!" he said, turning around.

"Indeed," said Jamuka, signalling the driver to pull in closer.

"Mum's never let me go in one. She says they're too dangerous."

He turned back to let NutNut continue filming.

"Be good, Bao Bao, until I return," said Jamuka, wrapping Nat up in a bear hug.

"I'll miss you," said Nat, fighting back the tears that came welling up.

He let go and sprang off the deck like a cat, dropping easily into the Rocketboat.

"Remember to look after Gobi," he shouted up.

Nat nodded. He waved. The driver opened up the throttle and the engines let out a deafening roar. The Rocketboat peeled away from the *Junko* at speed, its sparkling hull lifting up out of the water.

"Wow!" said Henry.

Nat didn't feel it was wow. Her heart felt heavy. Gobi started to chirp from her cage across the deck. She looked down at the star jar in her hands. Unscrewing the lid she peered in at the damp cloth containing the petal.

"Fizz, call Wen," she said.

Chapter Sixteen
WATCHEM

Nat stood Fizz on the sunken-deck dining table and flopped down on to the bench. His wings opened and Wen's face appeared on screen, grinning into camera. She'd had her fringe cut so it zigzagged across her forehead. Stranger still, her hair colour was now tangerine.

"*Heya*, Nat! Good timing. My shopping expedition with Granny Tang has just ended. Look!" She held up a huge gold bag. "Ronin jacket in here. Remember the one that was super *ding*? The one with the birds' wings on the back?" Her face disappeared from screen. "Wow. Mito jeans fifty per cent off."

"Jamuka's gone to the airport. He's going to Mongolia without me."

Wen's face popped back. "He's gone where?"

"Mongolia!" piped up Henry, jumping down next to Nat. "A big red petal arrived in a jar covered in stars. His Clan are sick, so he's had to go and help them!"

"Hey!" said Nat, pushing him out of camera.

"Are you serious?" said Wen.

Nat nodded. She held up the star jar so Wen could see it. "There's a weird red petal inside. Would your mum take a look at it?"

"*Ding* jar. I'll call her. She's at the lab. Hang on."

The screen went dark. The words "*On Hold*" started to flash across it.

"Yep. She can see you as long as you're quick," said Wen, reappearing. "She's got a meeting at two. Want me to meet you there?"

Nat breathed a sigh of relief. "Yes, please."

The Watchem Pharmaceutical Company was housed in a skyscraper on Po Wah Street. Its neon-pink sign hung over the main entrance. Nat pulled her Slider into the underground car park and found a spare parking slot. With Henry in tow she took the stairs up to the lobby and came out into a gleaming marble reception. A man in a white coat was standing behind the desk.

"We have an appointment with your chief scientist, Doctor Tang," said Nat. The man peered at them through thick bottle-end glasses.

"Names?" he said.

"Natalie and Henry Walker."

He picked up a lens from the desk. It was attached to a thin cable.

"Step forward. Look at camera."

"*Hai*, Lok. No need for that, they're with me," said Wen, cruising in through the main entrance on her Slider.

She parked up next to the desk, stepped off her board and tugged off her helmet. She put her head upside down to shake out her orange hair. "Follow me."

The doors to the lift swooshed closed. Wen hit the button for the fiftieth floor. "Now, tell me exactly what's going on."

By the time the doors opened into a long, brightly lit corridor, Nat had finished her story.

Wen let out a long, low whistle. "Wolves? Mana? It's like a movie. You know you can always come and stay with me."

"No, you should come and stay with me. We could hang out loads and I won't have to ride on Prissy's Slider," said Henry.

Nat really wanted to scowl at Henry but he looked so earnest that she folded her arms, nodding her head as if seriously weighing up his offer.

"That's really kind but I'm happy on the *Junko*

with Ah Wong."

Wen, who was already headed down the corridor, stopped in her tracks.

"*Ai yah!* That's impossible. Ah Wong's the most miserable person on the planet."

Nat shrugged. "Maybe, but I want to be at home, on the water."

As she walked along, Nat glanced at the digital advertising posters for Watchem's prescription drugs. In one, a boy on a bicycle was riding happily along a forest trail: "*Sacropill saved my life.*" A mother and baby on a park bench on a sunny summer's day: "*Without Watchem's Lifotabs I'd never see my baby grow up.*"

She paused, looking from the mother's smiling face to the gurgling baby in her arms. It was the life she had lost: the one in which her parents were alive, watching her grow up.

"Hurry up, Nat!" called Henry from the other end of the corridor.

Nat tore herself away from the poster and followed.

Chapter Seventeen
MYSTERY

Doctor Tang's office was sparsely furnished with a shiny desk and glass table surrounded by several metal chairs. It took a moment for Nat to recognise Wen's mother. At home, Doctor Tang wore Mito jeans, Sako shirts, bright-red lipstick and her long hair loose, swishing about her face. Today it was scraped back into a bun, and she was wearing a white lab coat and carrying protective glasses. She looked like a serious scientist.

"Lovely to see you, Nat," she said, giving her a hug.

"Anyone want a can of Popko?" said Wen, her head stuck inside a wall-mounted fridge in the corner.

"No, thanks," said Nat.

Ever since the package had arrived she hadn't felt the slightest bit hungry or thirsty.

"*Ku!*" Henry had his nose pressed up against a glass wall on the far side of the office.

Below lay a spotless room the size of a football field. Red and green buttons flashed on pieces of shining equipment. Scientists in lab coats were huddled over microscopes and Petri dishes.

Doctor Tang smiled. "The lab is where we do all our drug research and design. Now then," she said briskly. "I'm pressed for time, I'm afraid, so if you'd like to show me the petal I'll take a quick look."

Nat took the jar out of her backpack and placed it on the table. She unscrewed the top, pulled out the damp grey cloth and unfolded it to reveal the red petal.

"Oh, that would make a *ding* hair-colour combo," said Wen, seeing the deep red with electric blue.

Doctor Tang pushed a button. A snake light lowered from the ceiling, coming to rest just above the table. She pulled an eyepiece from her lab-coat pocket, along with a pair of transparent nano-gloves.

"Nat, please switch off your T-shirt so that it doesn't interfere with the light," she said.

"*Zoinks*, sorry," said Nat, reaching up to press the microdot sewn into the neck of her Smart T-shirt.

The kung fu-kicking *Scowler and the monster of Mars* movie scene that had been playing across the front vanished.

"This petal is unusual. Its texture feels rough, which is strange given its smooth appearance." Doctor Tang's voice was soft and precise. "The blue in it is surprising. I've never seen anything like it before."

She paused, staring hard at the petal as if trying to solve a puzzle.

"Scan," she commanded.

A clicking sound came from the overhead light. Doctor Tang looked up.

"I'm checking against our database now, which will tell us more," she said.

Nat caught sight of NutNut's head popping up out of Henry's shirt pocket. The squirrel's eyes snapped wide open, its ears turned, to record. She reached over and pushed its nose. NutNut disappeared back into Henry's pocket.

"No," she hissed.

Doctor Tang removed the eyepiece and peered at the petal. She pursed her lips tight together.

"Most strange. There is no match in our database and yet we have access to the Global Botanical Registry, which contains a record of every known species of plant. You say it came from Mongolia?"

Nat pointed at the star jar. "In this, through the post. The Clan wrote on the cloth that it came on the wind."

"Hey, maybe it blew in from outer space," said Wen, grinning.

Doctor Tang raised an eyebrow.

"Thank you, Wen."

"Well, you always say that we should be open to all theories, Mum."

Doctor Tang ignored her and turned the petal over in her fingers. "It's winter there now. Temperatures are sub-zero. The plant that this came from could not survive unless it was in a heated greenhouse."

"But Jamuka said his Clan live high up in the mountains and there's no one else around," said Nat.

"They're goat herders and they live in tents," added Henry.

Doctor Tang frowned. "Hmm, I see. To find out more I will need to do a chemical analysis on the petal."

"How long will that take?" asked Nat.

"A couple of days," said Doctor Tang, placing the petal into a clear sterile envelope.

A young laboratory technician in a white lab coat appeared through the door. Doctor Tang gave him a nod.

"Sorry, but I have to go. My meeting's about to start." She scraped back the chair and got to her feet. "As soon as I have news I'll be in touch, Nat."

Nat smiled, even though she didn't feel like it. She

didn't want to have to wait. She wanted to know the answer now. "Thank you."

Doctor Tang paused on her way to the door. "You girls have a sleepover tonight on the *Junko*, don't you? If Jamuka's away wouldn't it be better for you to come to our house?"

"Ah Wong's there to look after us," said Nat.

Doctor Tang smiled. "That's fine then. Wen, make sure you meet me at the dentist's tomorrow at ten sharp."

She walked out. Nat looked at the star jar on the table. The ear-piercing scream of the old woman in her nightmare replayed in her head. A chill ran through her. Deep down something inside told her this was only the beginning.

Chapter Eighteen
TUMEN VACHIR

They had just settled down to Ah Wong's tea on the upper deck of the *Junko* when Nat heard a familiar rattle of heavy bracelets.

"Yoohoo!"

Gobi started to chirp loudly from her perch.

"*Ai yah*, not the dragon mother," moaned Wen, looking up from the fashion pages she was viewing on Fu's screen.

"I thought Prissy was picking you up?" said Nat to Henry with a frown.

Henry shrugged, his mouth stuffed full of Ah Wong's cherry cake.

Nat pushed herself up from the cushions. The last thing she wanted was her aunt nosing around the boat.

"I'll intercept her. Hurry up and finish that, Henry. You've got to go."

She jumped down the wooden steps on to the main deck just as Aunt Vera appeared.

"My darling girl, when I heard the news from Prissy

I just had to come myself to see if there's anything I can do."

To both Nat's surprise and horror Aunt Vera opened her arms, drawing her into a bony embrace. Just when she thought she might suffocate from stinky Spice perfume she was released. Her aunt lifted her enormous owl-like sunglasses and peered closely at Nat's face.

"It's fine, thanks. Ah Wong's here," said Nat.

Aunt Vera raised an eyebrow. "How long is Jamuka going to be away?"

"Only a week at the most," she said, trying to make light of it. The last thing she wanted was her aunt interfering.

"And what kind of emergency is it? Prissy said something about a family matter?"

Nat waved a hand vaguely in the air. "Oh, just something to do with his aunt, that's all."

"And why didn't he take you with him?"

"Because it's deep winter there."

"Don't you think it might be better if you came to stay with us?"

Nat took a sharp intake of breath.

"No," she said quickly. "I want to be at home."

Henry came bounding across the deck.

"Hi, Mummy!" he said, thrusting NutNut under her nose. "Can I buy this?"

A striped Slider helmet was showing on NutNut's screen.

"No, darling."

"But Wen says it's the coolest thing that all *ding* boys are wearing."

"*Ding*? What an awful word. And the answer's still no."

"*Urgent call waiting from Mongolia*," announced Fizz from where he was standing, wings open, charging his solar batteries on the upper deck rail.

"I must take that," said Nat.

"Do you think it's about the pet—" began Henry, but before he could finish the sentence she pinched him on the arm. "Ow!"

"Not a word about anything," she hissed in his ear. She turned to Aunt Vera. "Please excuse me."

Her aunt nodded, her face full of concern. "Of course, darling girl. Now, do call us if there is anything, anything at all, that we can do."

"I will."

Nat sprinted across the deck, jumped up the steps and grabbed Fizz off the rail.

"Hello," she said, expecting Fizz to spread his

wings to reveal Jamuka on screen.

Instead there was nothing.

"Hello."

Still nothing. A wave of panic rose within her. The call had dropped. Jamuka had told her not to expect a call since he'd be out of any communication range already. So it could only mean one thing – bad news.

Nat felt something grasp her ankle. Looking down, she saw Fu's furry paws wrapped around her leg.

"Shhhh," said Wen, holding her finger to her mouth. She was lying flat on her stomach below sight level from the lower deck. "I thought you needed rescuing, so I called Fizz and told him to announce it was coming from Mongolia. Brainy move, eh?" she whispered.

Nat turned to see the top of Aunt Vera's super-sprayed helmet of blonde hair disappear down the gangplank. She bent down and lifted Fu up. The moment Fu was eye level with Fizz, the little dragon-robot started to purr. Fu's eyelids fluttered at his call.

"Stop that, Fizz! You're only meant to purr at me," said Nat, carrying them back over to the cushions.

Wen laughed. "I think they've had a crush on each other since we set them up to auto-greet."

"*Incoming call from Doctor Tang,*" announced Fizz.

"Take it and record call," Nat instructed.

"Looks like Mum's on the case," said Wen.

Fizz spread his wings. Doctor Tang appeared on screen. She was sitting at her office desk, wearing her white lab coat.

"Hello, Nat," she said. "Well, we've solved one part of the puzzle."

"Wow, that was quick."

Doctor Tang smiled.

"You have our lab technician, Tenko, to thank for the swift response. He decided to run a test for an uncommon chemical that occurs only in a rare plant found in Mongolia. The result came back positive for phyrosine kinase."

"Phyro what?"

"Phyrosine kinase. It is a reactor, a volatile chemical, very rare and hard to capture."

"What's the plant, Mum?" said Wen, leaning into camera next to Nat.

"Tumen Vachir, which roughly translates from Mongolian to 'ten thousand thunderbolts'."

Nat paused trying to take it all in. She'd have to get Fizz to play back the conversation later. Doctor Tang removed her glasses and pinched the bridge of her nose.

CRIMSON POISON

"What is it?" asked Wen.

Her mother lifted her hand, holding up a holographic 3D version of the petal. "This petal is ten times bigger and brighter than those on a normal Tumen Vachir plant. The electric-blue jagged line is something I have never seen before. That's why it didn't match the database. It's as if…" She paused. "As if someone's been interfering with its development."

"What do you mean?" said Nat.

Doctor Tang put her glasses back on.

"We're running more tests. I will know more tomorrow."

She ended the call. Nat stared at the blank screen. Jamuka's ashen face flashed through her mind. Was this the danger from outside, or the devastation within?

Chapter Nineteen
BETRAYAL

Wen left the *Junko* early the next morning. She'd forgotten to bring her new hair colour, which she needed to go with her tiger-striped outfit. Nat was left to eat breakfast alone. Rather than eat with a grumpy Ah Wong in the galley she took her plate of plum pancakes up on deck.

Overnight the weather had closed in. Thick, dark clouds coated the sky, making the harbour water below a choppy, gunmetal grey. The air had a knife-edged chill to it that cut through Nat's kimono. Her bare feet soaked up the cold dew that had settled on the wooden planks. All around smelled musty.

Gobi let out a low chirp from her cage, which hung on the mast.

"*Ai yah*, Gobi, I'm so sorry," said Nat, seeing the songbird's feathers fluffed up against the cold, her head buried underneath her wing.

She walked over and unhooked the cage.

"Sorry, but Wen couldn't stand you chirping all

night in the cabin." She shivered. Fat droplets of rain started to fall. "Let's head back to bed."

Even with the porthole closed it was cold. Nat pulled a thick woollen blanket out from underneath her bunk and placed it over her bed. She put Gobi's cage next to her and landed Fizz on top of it.

Gobi lifted her head and started to chirp through the bars at him. Fizz's eyes flashed red. He started to snort like a pig.

"Stop!" said Nat, moving him to the pillow.

She wondered where Jamuka had got to by now. There hadn't been a message from him since he'd left. She wondered what to do to fill the time. She could go to SPIN and try the next level with the Octozeb goggles, but she didn't want to miss Doctor Tang if she called. So she decided to do a long-put-off job – replacing two missing screws in her Slider helmet.

She opened a drawer in the shelf above her and took out a pair of magnifying glasses and a micro toolkit. She placed a new screw in the first hole and began to work it in. There was a flash of light, a sizzling sound. Fizz started to snort in alarm.

"*Zoinks!*" Nat dropped the screwdriver.

"*Use C-54 screw, not 84,*" said Fizz.

"Got it," she said.

A clattering of feet on the deck above broke her concentration.

"*Hai*, Nat!"

It was Henry. Strange. They hadn't made any plans. She heard the main hatch slide open and feet come running down the steps.

"I've got the best news," he said, bursting into her cabin. "Ooh, you look scary."

Nat removed her magnifying glasses.

"You're coming to stay with us!" he said, jumping on her bed.

"What?"

"Mummy's spoken with her lawyer. She's so worried that you're all on your own, and he says we can look after you until Jamuka returns. Isn't that *ku*?!"

Nat dropped the helmet. It clattered on to the floorboards.

"She's done what?"

"We can be a big happy family. Well, Prissy's not pleased about it, of course, but I am. We can have so much fun!"

He bounced up and down on the mattress. Gobi's cage rocked wildly, nearly knocking her off her perch. She screeched.

"Stop!" said Nat, pushing him off the bed.

"Ouch!" said Henry, skidding on the rug. "That wasn't very nice."

"I'm not going anywhere. This is my home, and Ah Wong's here."

"Mummy says it's great that Daddy and her are your family guardians so they can help you and you won't be alone."

Nat leapt off the bed.

"Where is she?"

Henry shrugged. "I don't know. She followed me up the gangplank."

Nat grabbed Fizz and marched down the corridor. She could hear voices in the galley. Walking in, she found Aunt Vera handing over a large brown envelope to Ah Wong. Ah Wong's normally miserable face had cracked into a crooked smile.

"What's going on?" said Nat.

"Darling girl!" said Aunt Vera, spinning round on a spiky stiletto heel. "I'm sending Ah Wong on a long-deserved holiday back to her family in Dazhou and you're coming to stay with us. We're going to have such fun!"

Blood thundered in Nat's ears. Her face turned bright red.

"You can't do that!"

"Your Uncle Fergal and I are so worried that you won't be properly looked after that we think it's best you come to stay with us while Jamuka's missing. We are, after all, your real family."

"Missing? He's not missing, he's gone to see his aunt."

Aunt Vera held up a white envelope in her bony hand.

"Precisely. He went to see his family but he sadly seems to have gone missing. My lawyer has tried repeatedly to contact him about your welfare, but there has been no response. So we thought it best to make it formal."

Nat snatched the envelope from her aunt, tore it open and pulled out a single-page document. It was a Hong Kong Court filing paper bearing today's date and a time of eight thirty a.m.

She scanned it quickly, her tears blurring the words. She slammed the paper on the galley kitchen table. Ah Wong and Aunt Vera jumped in surprise.

"How dare you!" she screamed. "How dare you do this to me?"

Fizz's eyes flashed red and smoke started to spurt out of his nostrils right into Aunt Vera's face.

CRIMSON POISON

"Stop that now!" she said, wafting the air with her hand.

But Fizz didn't. Aunt Vera was forced to step back towards the sink.

"I'm not going to do what this says," said Nat, slapping her hand down on top of the document. "You can't make me."

A thin smile spread across Aunt Vera's lips.

"Darling girl. You don't have a choice, I'm afraid. If you don't come with us then I shall be forced to call the police and report you as a runaway child."

Chapter Twenty
TRAITOR

Nat wiped the tears from her face with the back of her hand and shoved the last of her clothes into her already overstuffed ancient suitcase. She pushed down the top but it refused to close. Henry obliged by sitting on it. This was fast becoming a nightmare. She'd sent ten SOS messages to Jamuka. Wen was busy at the dentist and didn't answer. She'd no one else to turn to.

Aunt Vera swished in through the door. "Now, don't pack too much as I've got lots of pretty things that Prissy has outgrown."

There was no way Nat would ever wear anything of Prissy's. She would rather wear a rubbish bag than parade around in a neon-coloured dress.

"And do hurry up. Prissy's show is in twenty minutes. I'll see you up on deck. Chop-chop!"

"We're going to have a wicked time," said Henry.

Nat didn't reply. She couldn't. Everything inside her felt wrung out and empty. She lifted Fizz on to her shoulder and dragged her suitcase on its three rusty wheels across the cabin floor to the door. Gobi chirped. She turned back to Henry.

"Bring Gobi, please."

"*Ku!*" said Henry. "I've always wanted a pet but Mummy's never allowed me to have one."

Aunt Vera was up on deck speaking quickly to Ah Wong, who was making notes on a pad of paper.

"Henry, leave that here, please," she said, seeing the birdcage.

"But Jamuka wants me to look after her," said Nat.

"Ah Wong, that's another thing for your list. Remove bird."

"No!" said Nat, snatching the cage from Henry. "She's Jamuka's songbird. She has to come with me."

Aunt Vera tapped her toe impatiently on the deck.

"My word is final. Remove bird."

Nat narrowed her eyes. She walked up to Ah Wong and handed her the cage.

"Please take her to Mr Choi and ask him to look after her until Jamuka returns."

Ah Wong nodded, not looking up at her.

"Traitor," said Nat under her breath so that only Ah Wong would hear. "You'll pay dearly for this."

Chapter Twenty-One
THE CUTTING

The wind whined and shrieked through the trees. The man hugged his long coat around him and stepped out of the tent. The icy night air made his breath crackle and his face freeze. His head was filled with images from his nightmare: the tiger, its claws poised to slice through his sweat-soaked body. It was better to be up and awake.

He set off across the snowy wasteland, his head bowed against the wind. The thin sliver of moon cast an eerie glow over the compound. Reaching the first greenhouse he took out his key and unlocked the door. As he stepped inside, the warm scent of soil and vegetation hit his nostrils. The constant hum of the generators replaced the howl of the wind. Pots of leafy plants filled the space like a jungle. He paced down the first row, checking each plant.

"*Ugui,*" he said.

The green buds had sprouted but not one had unfurled into the blooming red flower he was so

CRIMSON POISON

desperate to see. Time was running out.

He reached into his pocket and pulled out a penknife. His hands trembled as he bent over a plant and sliced off a bud. Holding it up to a bright lamp, he tried to hold his hands steady as he drew the blade through it. His sweaty fingers slipped on the handle and the blade cut into the soft flesh of his thumb.

"Argh," he cried, blood spilling from the gash.

The knife clattered to the ground. He grabbed an old piece of cloth and bound it tightly around his thumb to try and staunch the flow. He should not have meddled with the secret. Perhaps this was an omen.

Anger swelled at his clumsiness. He grabbed a pair of thick rubber gloves and a face mask from a hook. Reaching beneath a table, he pulled out a barrel, took the hose, which snaked out of the top, and twisted the valve. A fine spray showered the leaves and buds.

On the side of the barrel was a large skull and crossbones along with a bright-green label: *Growemup Fertiliser – makes your plants grow like rockets!*

The plants would grow stronger and more powerful than ever. The Clan would get another dose of poison. He felt better already.

Chapter Twenty-Two
SHAN-XI

After an excruciating hour watching Prissy's dance troupe practise their hip-hop-tap-fusion show, Aunt Vera took them on a shopping trip. Nat's biggest fear was that someone would spot her entering Shan-xi's pink and gold doors. She had never been in a luxury store like this and she didn't like it one bit.

"Mrs Walker, how good to see you!" A female assistant wobbled over on a pair of gold platform heels.

They air-kissed.

"Prissy, that hot-pink jacket has just come in."

Prissy squealed, "*Ku!*" and clapped her hands together.

Nat saw that Henry had already manoeuvred his way on to a zebra-striped sofa where he was busy playing a game of *Fire Frog* on NutNut. Nat was about to perch herself next to him, when the assistant's *you-need-new-clothes* radar detected her.

"Oh," she said, taking in Nat's dragon T-shirt, cargo

shorts and Slider boots. "Is this the, er, problem you called me about, Mrs Walker?"

Aunt Vera smiled and raised her eyes. "Yes, well, you can see what I mean."

Nat felt like a cornered rat. She tried to back off towards the door but was grabbed by Aunt Vera and steered firmly towards the assistant.

"I don't need new clothes."

"Nonsense. A girl your age needs to start dressing properly. You can't be a tomboy forever. Mei here is kindly going to help."

Two other assistants appeared out of nowhere. One scooped up Nat and shoved her into a changing room while the other girl pulled things off the rails. The clothes were bright pink, lime green, fluorescent yellow, silver and gold.

"She's the heir to the Walker SPIN fortune," Aunt Vera smiled.

Nat cringed while Mei and the assistant looked at her with renewed interest, dollar signs in their eyes as they absorbed the fact that she was heiress to one of the most successful computer games companies in the world.

In the corner of the changing room Aunt Vera perched on the edge of a heart-shaped satin chair.

Mei stood arms folded at the entrance. There was no escape. Nat placed Fizz on a glass table and shyly removed her T-shirt and shorts.

"Goodness me, you can't wear those!" Aunt Vera clapped her hand over her mouth.

The mirrors showed Nat's faded grey vest and an old pair of school pants, minus their elastic, held together with a safety pin. Nat closed her eyes. *Please, please, please make all this go away.*

Mei clicked her fingers. The assistant popped her head round the door. "Does she want to try it in citrus?" she asked, while Aunt Vera fanned herself with the latest Shan-xi brochure.

To her eternal shame, Nat was released from the changing room in a hot-pink dress emblazoned with the signature "S" on the front. Her silver mules clattered as she tilted precariously, unable to walk in a straight line. Her new underwear was tight and itchy. At Aunt Vera's insistence, Nat had reluctantly picked out several hideous new outfits, and her old clothes and boots had been sent off with the assistant for disposal.

Henry's eyes popped out when he saw her. "You look just like Prissy!"

"So do you," Nat muttered furiously.

CRIMSON POISON

Mei presented the bill to Aunt Vera, who said, "Deliver everything to us at Wetley Towers, but send the bill to Walker Trust at SPIN." She grabbed a very expensive jewelled purse off a nearby table and handed it to Mei. "I'll take this too. It will go with everything."

Nat gulped. Her new wardrobe, Prissy's new shoes and clothes, and Aunt Vera's new bag would add up to a small fortune. She opened her mouth to say something but realised it was useless. Wait until she told Jamuka.

Chapter Twenty-Three
KIMONO

By the time they reached Wetley Towers it was late. Aunt Vera was in a panic because she had six coming for supper. Ming was already in the kitchen boiling up a vat of rice for Aunt Vera's Chicken 21.

Nat kicked off her mules and ran along the marble hallway to her room. The lampshade was mauve, the carpet lilac, the walls aubergine and the bedcover violet. It was like a purple padded cell. She knelt on the floor and opened her suitcase. Her stomach lurched. She gasped in horror; all the clothes she had packed were gone. Only her sponge bag remained, and the star jar. She leapt up and opened the wardrobe door. It was empty except for a purple dressing gown. She pulled open every drawer; the entire chest of drawers was empty.

In a split second she was in the brightly lit turquoise dining room where Aunt Vera was supervising Ming as she laid the table.

"Where are my clothes?" she demanded. "What

have you done with them?"

Aunt Vera looked up disapprovingly. "Nat, I insist you keep your voice down. I asked Ming to remove them so there's room for your new wardrobe."

"You did what?" Nat's voice was shrill and shaky.

"It's for the best. You have to grow up."

Nat's eyes narrowed. "Give them back, now, please." She forced the words out. "You have no right—"

"I will not be spoken to like that," said Aunt Vera. By now both Henry and Prissy were standing in the doorway. "You are staying under my roof and I am your guardian…"

Nat clenched her fists together. "Temporary guardian."

"This means that you will respect and obey my wishes."

Nat took a deep breath. "Please, Aunt Vera, where are my things?"

Aunt Vera looked over at Ming. "Would you like to explain?"

Ming did not look at Nat as she spoke. She kept her eyes fixed on the dining-room table. She spoke quickly, the words darting out like poisoned needles. "I put them down the chute to the incinerator, like Mrs Walker said."

Nat felt faint. She grabbed hold of the back of a chair for support. For a moment she was speechless.

"How could you do that? My mother's kimono was in there. Did you burn that as well?"

Ming shrugged. "Mrs Walker said everything."

Silence hung hot and heavy in the room. Nat glared at Aunt Vera. "I'll never, ever forgive you for this."

Chapter Twenty-Four
SUPPER FOR SIX

Nat refused to eat supper. She stayed in her room. The purple swags above the four-poster bed billowed in the breezy air conditioning. It was late now and she could hear laughter as Aunt Vera's supper party moved into full swing. Uncle Fergal was telling a terrible joke about a dog and a tree. A chair scraped back from the table.

"Time for a brandy snifter, I think," said Uncle Fergal.

Nat heard his heavy footsteps in the hallway as he headed to the kitchen. There was a lull in the conversation.

"So, Vera, how long is your niece staying with you?" came a woman's voice.

"With Jamuka gone, I should think she'll be here for some time."

Nat put her ear to the door.

"How kind of you to take her in."

"Just in time." Aunt Vera sounded smug. "She

needs her real family around her. She has no female influence in her life at all. Can you imagine? You know, of course, that she lost her parents at a horribly young age."

"A car accident, wasn't it?"

"Plane. They were on their way back from a conference in Taiwan when a freak electrical storm broke out. The tail of the SPIN jet was struck by lightning. The plane went down. There were no survivors." Aunt Vera paused for effect. It was evidently a story she had told many times before. She waited for everyone to gasp. "They had nearly taken Nat with them but it was such a quick day trip they left her at home. Imagine, oh just imagine, if she had been with them too?"

Nat thought how pleased Aunt Vera would have been if she had been on the plane. She and Uncle Fergal would have stood to inherit the entire SPIN empire.

"How wonderful for her to have some proper mothering, Vera," said the woman.

"I have my work cut out for me. She can be difficult, you know. I think she's been a little too indulged."

Nat felt like opening the door and marching in to set the record straight, but she was beaten to it by

Uncle Fergal, who clomped back down the hallway with his prized bottle of brandy.

"A tipple of my finest for everyone?" he said, landing it with a clang on the glass-topped table.

There was a murmur of consent and the conversation turned to the latest gossip at the country club.

Nat had never felt more alone or powerless. Being under Aunt Vera's roof was even worse than she could ever have imagined.

"*Incoming call from Wen,*" announced Fizz.

"Take it."

His wings spread and there was Wen on the screen, bouncing up and down with very loud rock music playing in the background. One moment her head was visible, next it was her red shirt.

"*Hai,* Nat!" she shouted. "Check out these bounding boots." She lifted a foot up to show a black boot with a spring-loaded heel. "*Ding* or what?" The foot disappeared, replaced by a beaming face.

"Where have you been?"

"Straight after the dentist Mum took me on a surprise trip to see the new Mito collection up in Shenzhen. I couldn't take Fu with me because they wouldn't allow any filming. We've only just got back. So what's up? I've got an all-time-record fifteen missed calls from you."

Nat took a deep breath. "Aunt Vera's got a court order making her and Uncle Fergal my guardians until Jamuka returns and I've had to move into their apartment. Worse still, Aunt Vera's burned my mother's kimono."

The bouncing stopped. Wen turned the music off.

"*Ai yah!* That witch! I'm coming straight over to jump on her in my boots. Tell me everything."

Chapter Twenty-Five
ESCAPE

Without the rocking motion of the *Junko*, Nat tossed and turned, unable to sleep. Aunt Vera's dinner party had finished and the raucous laughter had been replaced with the hum of the air conditioning. She'd watched a couple of old film clips of her parents but instead of helping her fall asleep as usual, this time they'd only made her feel more alone than ever before.

She kicked off the sheet and switched on the bedside lamp.

"Let's get out of here, Fizz," she said, picking up the hideous pink Shan-xi dress off the floor.

Fizz's eyes snapped open for an instant, before closing again.

"*It is three o'clock in the morning. Sleep time,*" he announced.

"It may be three, but you need to wake up. I'm not staying in vile Vera's purple guest box any longer. We're going back home."

She tugged the dress over her head and grabbed her kung fu slippers from underneath the bed. At least Ming hadn't been able to find them.

"*Not safe outside; too late at night*," said Fizz.

"Well, we're going out anyway and we're going to sail far away from all this until Jamuka comes back."

She took the star jar out from underneath her pillow and put it in her backpack. Looking around the room she realised there was nothing else left of hers to take; the rest was now ash. Picking up Fizz she headed for the door.

"Switch to silent mode, Fizz."

Out in the hallway she could hear a deep rumbling snore coming from Uncle Fergal and Aunt Vera's room. That would provide good cover. She tiptoed along to the kitchen and quietly turned the door handle. It was dark inside except for the digital glow of the fridge readout. Underneath the sink she could see the outline of Ming, sound asleep in her narrow bunk. She held her breath as she passed by, terrified Ming would wake up and raise the alarm.

The door clicked shut behind her. She'd made it out into the apartment block corridor. She took off at a run like a rat from a sinking ship. Rather than wait for the lift, she decided to run down the emergency stairs, taking three at time, to reach the underground car park. She pulled her Slider out of the rack, crammed on her helmet and thrust the handlebars forward. She zoomed up the ramp and out into the warm Hong Kong night.

The Slider lanes were quiet. She soon arrived at the Causeway Bay Royal Yacht Club. Fizz scanned her in through the owners' entrance and she headed across the lawns, the smell of the saltwater in the air calming her ragged nerves.

She passed the line of super-yachts and headed out to the end of the jetty. But when she got to the last mooring, it was empty.

"Where is it?" she said, looking out across the marina, searching for the *Junko*'s signature three masts.

She lifted Fizz up off the handlebars.

"Fizz, locate home."

Fizz's eyes lit up bright green. He lifted his snout up into the air as his GPS system searched.

"Junko *is in transit headed towards Shelter Cove, New Territories.*"

The words hit Nat like a tsunami.

"What? That's miles away. Call Ah Wong," she said.

"*No reply. Cuts to auto-answer. Leave message?*"

She slammed her hand down hard on the handlebars.
"No! Cut to DeckCam."

Fizz's wings opened. Nat expected to see an immediate live feed from the *Junko*'s deck. Instead the screen showed the black and grey snow of a dead connection.

"*Data feed disabled.*"

"Try every JunkoCam."

"*All data feeds disabled.*"

Nat clutched her stomach and sank down on to her board. Her home was gone. The world she knew was being ripped away from her.

"Call Henry."

Henry appeared on Fizz's screen. His hair was standing on end. He yawned and sleepily rubbed his eyes.

"Nat?" he said. "Are you outside?"

"Yes. I'm where the *Junko* was and it isn't here any more. Do you know anything about it?"

Henry bit his lip.

"Oh dear," he said.

Nat sighed. "What? Tell me."

"Mum paid Ah Wong fifty thousand dollars to take it away. It was all in cash; she counted it out on the kitchen table before we came to get you from the

Junko. It was a mountain of notes. I saw Prissy hide a few of them in her pocket."

"WHAT? That's a fortune! Why didn't you tell me before?"

Henry winced. His face turned as red as Popko juice. Nat wanted to reach through the camera and punch him, lash out at him for not letting her know before. Instead she leapt up and high-kicked her handlebars. She hit them with such force that the Slider went into a tailspin, whizzing round and round like a spinning top, her and Fizz with it.

Fizz started to snort in alarm. Smoke poured out of his snout. Nat jammed her foot on to the ground, bringing them to an abrupt halt.

"I'm so sorry. Mummy made me promise not to say anything to you. She said she'd take NutNut off me for a year if I did," said Henry.

Nat took a deep breath. She'd never really hated someone before.

"The witch! That's two years' wages for Ah Wong. Is she sailing the *Junko* up to Shelter Cove as part of the deal?"

Henry's shoulders slumped. "I think so."

"What else? Come on, what else has she done?"

Nat leaned into camera. Her nostrils flared, her eyes

wide with fury. Henry jumped back in fright.

"I don't know. That's all I heard. Please come back home. If Mummy wakes up and finds you gone she'll call the police."

Chapter Twenty-Six
ROBOT DOCTOR

Nat sat on the jetty staring out into the dark waters of Victoria Harbour. A cold wind cut through her thin Shan-xi dress but she was oblivious to it. She was a hollow shell, a dry husk of a girl, her soul sucked out by her wicked aunt.

She wondered if she should go to Wen's, but that would more than likely make things worse. Aunt Vera was bound to track her down and drag her back.

After leaving a very long message for Jamuka, which she could only hope he might pick up, she climbed aboard her Slider and made her way slowly back to Wetley Towers.

Dawn was breaking when she pulled into the car park. She took the lift up and decided to enter through the apartment's front door in case Ming was already awake and at work in the kitchen.

She quietly opened the door and began to creep down the hallway.

"You are in big trouble," said Prissy, appearing at

the doorway to her bedroom in a satin dressing gown and seaweed face mask.

Nat scowled at her and broke into a run towards the purple guest room but she was blocked by Aunt Vera coming out from the kitchen. "And just where have you been?"

Nat stared at her in horror. Aunt Vera was wearing a silver nano-mesh hairnet and her face was frozen with a thick layer of night-time Cementer.

"I wanted to get some air," she said.

"Liar! You were going to the *Junko*, weren't you? Henry said you were trying to escape."

Henry? How could he have told her that?

"Well, I couldn't, could I? You got Ah Wong to sail it away. That's my home you've taken, and you've no right to!" said Nat, her fists clenched at her sides.

Aunt Vera took a step towards her. The smell of sour coffee on her breath made Nat gag. She raised a long bony finger and stabbed it at Nat's chest. "You are a spoiled, selfish little orphan and you are banned from going out again – without me."

Fizz's high-pitched alarm rang out.

"Stop that thing," said Aunt Vera, whipping Nat's pack off her shoulder.

CRIMSON POISON

She ripped open the top and thrust her hand inside.

"Agh!" she screamed, pulling out her hand with Fizz hanging from a finger by a claw. "Get it off me."

Nat didn't move. She was delighted that her aunt had activated Fizz's anti-theft protection.

"Get it off me! Now!" she screamed.

Nat cupped Fizz in her hand. The moment he sensed her, he released Aunt Vera's finger.

"I will go to my room now," said Nat, her voice low and cold.

Aunt Vera's eyes narrowed. She held out her hand.

"Give that to me now."

"No!" said Nat, holding Fizz protectively to her chest.

"Or else I shall call the robot doctor and have him taken apart piece by piece."

Nat swallowed hard. She knew her aunt well enough to know that if she didn't hand him over, she would lose him forever.

"Be good," she whispered to Fizz, and flicked the switch under his wing to power him down. His eyes closed, his wings whirred to a close. "If you hurt him I'll make sure you pay."

Aunt Vera's claw-like hand snatched the dragon.

"He's a robot, for goodness' sake. Now, get out of

my sight," she said, turning on her spiky heels and marching off towards her room.

Nat fled to her bedroom, closed the door and collapsed on the bed. Her blood boiled with anger and frustration.

An hour later she was lying on the bed staring up at the lilac ceiling when she saw something slide out from underneath the door. Looking down she saw a slip of paper lying on the floor. She reached down and picked it up. It was a hand-scrawled note from Henry:

Dear Nat, I am very sorry but Mummy overhurd me talking to you. She was sneeking at my door and when we stopped talking she came in and took NutNut from me. I hate her like you do. You are lucky that she is not your mummy and Prissy is not your sisster. I am banned to my room but tiptowed down to give you this. We are in prizon. I miss NutNut. Very sorry agane. Henry.

A faint smile passed her lips. At least Henry wasn't a traitor after all. She sat up. She would go and see him. The chances of getting caught were slim since she was sure Aunt Vera would be leaving them to suffer for at least another few hours.

She was barefoot, halfway down the hallway, when she heard loud, stage-like whispers coming from the kitchen.

"What do you mean, you didn't get the promotion?" said Aunt Vera.

"They gave it to Lee," said Uncle Fergal.

Nat was about to continue onwards towards Henry's room when Aunt Vera let out an ear-piercing screech, rooting Nat to the spot.

"Lee? You've been at the bank fifteen years longer than him. All those dinner parties I've hosted to push you up the ladder and it all amounts to nothing. You should be president now. Instead you're a middle manager on a salary that wouldn't keep a mouse in clothes."

Nat gasped. She might not like Uncle Fergal but he didn't deserve that.

A hand rapped down on the table. "There I was thinking I was marrying a man with means. And what's it come to? Nothing!"

"And who do you think pays for this lavish lifestyle of yours, the club, the flat, the clothes, Prissy and Henry's education, the dinner parties?" Uncle Fergal protested.

Nat could hear Aunt Vera suck in the air between

her teeth like a hissing cobra. "We scrape through each month on your meagre salary. And don't you forget we've taken out a big loan to keep it all rolling until you get a promotion. And look where we are now – no promotion! We're going to be destitute."

Uncle Fergal let out a loud sigh. "We'll just have to make some cutbacks until the next round of promotions is announced."

"No. We will not. I refuse to be a pauper. There's only one thing for it. We'll just have to secure the Brat's guardianship."

Nat felt like running in and giving her aunt a high kick.

"Well, you'd better make sure you do it fast then, after all the money you've spent since she arrived. These bills are outrageous!"

Nat heard papers being shuffled and snatched.

"I've been scrimping for long enough, Fergal. You can't keep me in the manner that I expect, so I will sort it out myself."

Uncle Fergal's heavy footsteps echoed along the hallway. Nat turned and fled to her room. She made it through the door just as he came thundering out, red-faced and sweating.

There was a loud slam of the front door then all

went deadly quiet. The efficient click of Aunt Vera's stilettos came next. Nat held her breath as they paused outside her door. There was a brisk knock and Aunt Vera's head appeared around the door.

Nat turned away.

"Darling girl, how are you?" said Aunt Vera, her voice silky.

She sat down next to Nat on the bed and placed a hand over hers in a firm grip. "I'm sorry I was angry earlier. I was just so concerned that you might have been kidnapped. But I'd like us to forget the whole matter."

Nat swallowed hard and turned to face her. Aunt Vera was wearing the same pink dress as her. Her stick-thin arms, draped in gold bangles, looked even more ridiculous with her blonde mushroom hair sticking out on top.

"And here's your darling dragon," she said, placing Fizz in Nat's lap.

Nat picked him up. The normally warm scales were cold. His eyes were closed.

"Now, I must leave shortly to attend a special meeting. Prissy's off to see Candy in a few minutes, it's Ming's day off, so can I leave you with Henry to just hang out together? Maybe you could go for a fun Slamburger."

She tried to wink at Nat but her face was so frozen with Cementer that it looked more like a nervous twitch. Before Nat could reply, Aunt Vera leaned over and pecked her on the forehead.

"*Ku!*" she said, standing up and noticing Nat's dress. "We're twins."

A lingering whiff of perfume was left in her wake as she walked out of the door. Nat rubbed her eyes. She was tired from lack of sleep, and even more tired from the whirlwind of emotions that surfaced every time she saw her aunt.

She reached beneath Fizz's wing to power him up. His eyes flashed bright green.

"*Message from Doctor Tang.*"

Chapter Twenty-Seven
MARBOLIC

Nat, Wen and Henry raced through the doors into the Watchem lobby.

"*Hai*, Lok. Is Mum in the lab?" said Wen, running towards the lift.

"Yes, you're expected," he said.

"Wen, darling," said Doctor Tang, giving her daughter a hug as she raced in. She glanced over her shoulder and saw Nat and Henry hovering inside the door. "Nat, Henry. Come in and sit down. Wen told me you are staying at your aunt and uncle's, Nat."

Nat nodded. Doctor Tang put her hand on Nat's arm.

"I know family can be difficult, but I am sure they have your best interests at heart."

Nat bit her lip. Part of her wanted to spill out the whole sorry story straightaway, but she decided to wait until after she'd found out why they had been urgently called in.

"Now." Wen's mum became businesslike. "Our

tests show the petal contains traces of a very rare poison."

"Poison?" said Nat, suddenly alert. Had Jamuka arrived to find his Clan and the wolf pack dead? Was he still alive?

"Marbolic," said Doctor Tang. "I first came across it several years ago during the Growemup scandal. Growemup was a fertiliser used to speed up growth and strengthen plants. They discovered that the chemical compounds in Growemup reacted with certain plants to form a deadly poison. The scientists called it Marbolic. Once it was discovered, Growemup was banned."

Nat shuddered. She reached into her pocket and pressed Fizz's snout to record. Doctor Tang pressed a button on the table.

Henry's face wrinkled up as a hologram of a mouse appeared in mid-air before them.

"*Ai yah!* Mum!" said Wen, turning away.

The mouse's eyes had popped out like marbles.

"Marbolic attacks the central nervous system. Smaller doses can cause severe fatigue, and ingested in larger quantities it leads to paralysis, muscle failure and eventually death."

"Is there a cure?" asked Nat.

CRIMSON POISON

"Some research has been done, but to date no one has discovered an antidote." Doctor Tang switched off the screen. "It appears the Tumen Vachir plant is being fertilised with Growemup. I've contacted the Mongolian authorities, as this is a potential environmental disaster. Since they haven't received reports from any other sources, and they're short-staffed with the new government-funding cuts, they will only take action if we can verify and locate the source. To do that we must find Jamuka and his Clan."

Nat gulped. Did Jamuka know all this? Or was this something new?

"All I know is that they're in the mountains somewhere."

Doctor Tang got to her feet and started to pace the office, her hands clasped behind her back. "Is there a village nearby that we can get word to?"

Nat ran through Jamuka's old bedtime stories. "Maybe somewhere in the Hentii Mountains?"

Doctor Tang called up a map of Mongolia from the table computer. A holographic map floated above the table. It zoomed into the Hentii Mountains. "This is a massive area. Where exactly?" she asked.

Tree-filled mountain slopes, lakes and grassy plains filled a vast landscape that seemed to stretch forever.

There were no buildings, roads or anything that could be identified as a distinctive landmark.

"The Clan are nomadic," said Nat. "Jamuka says they move with the seasons."

Then a name popped into her head, recalled from a long-ago conversation with her guardian. "Qadan. Q-A-D-A-N."

"Search for Qadan," commanded Doctor Tang.

"*Qadan not known,*" replied the computer.

Nat frowned. "Maybe it's not this part of the Hentii Mountains after all."

They searched further afield for a while but could find nothing.

Doctor Tang shook her head and tutted. "We need more information about this plant, and fast."

They all fell silent, the weight of the situation sinking in. Doctor Tang removed her glasses.

"I have an idea. I'll get in touch with my old colleague Doctor Fred Fairlight. She specialises in new plants that have been crossbred from existing ones and knows all about fertilisers and their impact on the environment. We travelled to the Amazon together last year. If anyone could find the antidote, it's Fred."

Doctor Tang brought up her contact list on the

table screen. A large red X was marked next to Doctor Fred Fairlight. To the right was a short update:

I am currently on expedition in Borneo and won't be checking messages for six months. When funds run out, I will return. Don't leave a message. I cannot pick it up.

Doctor Tang sighed. "Typical Fred. There's only one thing for it, you need to find Jamu—"

A loud beeping alarm began to sound across the room. Doctor Tang jumped to her feet and ran for the door.

"I have to go, there's an emergency in the lab. We'll talk later."

Chapter Twenty-Eight
HUNTING BORJIGINS

Henry let out a long burp across Wen's kitchen.

He grinned. "That was the best Popko juice ever. Can I have another one?"

"No, we've got to get to work on finding Jamuka," said Nat, tapping Fizz's head. His wings spread to reveal the screen. "The Clan's last name is Borjigin, so if we search for them in Mongolia we might be able to find a contact number and get a message to them. Find Borjigin, Mongolia, Fizz."

Fizz's eyes flashed bright green. A list of Borjigin names started to spool on to the screen.

"Catch!" said Wen.

"Can you get your robots to work, please?" said Nat, glancing up to see her throwing another can of ice-cold Popko "Celebration" to Henry.

"Fu, find Borjigins in Mongolia pronto!" shouted Wen at her rabbit, who was lying in the sun at the window getting a quick solar charge. Fu squeaked loudly and thumped her foot on the window ledge.

CRIMSON POISON

"Please!" shouted Wen.

"*Polite request accepted. Searching Borjigins, Mongolia.*"

Wen growled. "That rabbit can be so annoying."

"*List complete. One hundred and fifty-three thousand, six hundred and twelve Borjigins listed in Mongolia,*" announced Fizz.

Nat put her head down on the kitchen worktop and groaned. "*Zoinks!* That's way too many."

"We've got three robots so if we divide it by three it's a lot less," said Henry, burping again.

Wen started jumping up and down in a pair of bounding boots. With the spring-loaded heels she was flying up so high that her spiky hair was grazing the ceiling.

"No, I've got it. Fu, pleeeeeeeeeze do another search for Borjigins in the Hentii Mountains."

Fu's furry ears pricked up, she squeaked and started searching. Seconds later she announced, "*Borjigins in Hentii Mountains is a null search.*"

Nat rubbed her eyes. They felt gritty and sore. Just looking at the endless list on Fizz's screen made her heart sink. Wen appeared at her side, bouncing up and down.

"You're making me dizzy."

Wen jumped up and sat down on the kitchen worktop next to her.

"I think well when I bound. Drives Mum mad too. But it gets results. As Henry says, there are three robots, so let's start one off at the top of the list, one in the middle and one from the bottom up."

"Doing what?" said Nat.

"They can auto-call-up the contact numbers listed."

"But what do they do when someone answers?" said Henry, tipping the last drops from the Popko can into his mouth.

Nat looked out of the huge window with its multimillion-dollar view down from The Peak, across Victoria Harbour. A grey shroud of sea fog hung low over the water, blocking out Kowloon in the distance.

"Hmm … something about the Clan," said Wen.

Nat sat up in her seat. She picked up Fizz. He purred as she cradled him in her hand.

"Great idea. We can set them up with a script, auto-translated into Mongolian, which asks if they know the Borjigin Clan in the Hentii Mountains. If they do then Fizz, Fu or NutNut asks them to hold, they alert us and then we speak to the Borjigin through auto-translate!"

Wen grinned. "*Ding* logical thinking! Your dad

would have been proud of you."

"Thanks," said Nat, her voice soft.

Wen jumped down and bounded over to Fu.

"He was a legend. When you become one too, just don't forget me."

"Or me. Here," said Henry, handing her NutNut. "NutNut, allow Fizz to link all."

The squirrel's ears twitched. She swivelled her head around to locate Fizz and her eyes lit up bright yellow.

"And here's the big bunny for you," said Wen, landing Fu on the worktop. "Fu, allow Fizz to link all."

A paw thumped on the polished wooden surface.

"Please," said Wen.

Nat worked hard perfecting and programming the script while Wen decided to design Henry a new T-shirt, declaring the one he was wearing as *un-ding* and dull.

"Done!" said Nat a long while later.

She climbed off the high stool, stretching her arms above her head. On the worktop stood the dragon, squirrel and rabbit in a circle. They were motionless except for their glowing eyes. Inside each one of them their circuits were buzzing, working at lightning speed, auto-dialling contact numbers, reading the script and processing the replies.

Nat looked around the kitchen. She was the only one there. Outside, fat droplets of rain were streaming down the windows.

She left the robots working and wandered across the kitchen, out into the vast marble hallway. Paintings of Wen's fearsome ancestors glared down at her from the walls. She stepped on to the priceless silk rug and headed up the sweeping staircase to Wen's room.

"The search is underway," she said, finding Wen and Henry peering into Wen's 3D printer. A black-and-purple-striped sleeve was slowly appearing in the output tray.

"*Ai yah!* I've forgotten to add the squirrel to the sleeves!" said Wen, pulling the printer plug out of the wall.

"Why did you do that?" said Henry with a frown.

Wen pulled the half-knitted sleeve from the tray. "It's the only way to stop it."

"The search has started," repeated Nat.

Henry and Wen turned to her, wide-eyed.

"For the Borjigins," said Nat, flopping down on to Wen's bed. Her head sank into a soft feather-filled pillow. "For the Borjig…" She gave a huge yawn.

Chapter Twenty-Nine
SARAWAK TOURS

A sharp, smoky smell made Nat wake with a start. She opened her eyes to find Wen waving a steaming cup underneath her nostrils.

"Good, you're awake. Drink," she said, putting the cup to her friend's lips.

Nat took a sip.

"Urgh!" she said, sitting up. "What is it?"

Wen grinned. "Vietnamese weasel coffee. Mum had some in the cupboard."

Nat's hand flew to her mouth. "Yuk!"

"It's the only way I could get you to wake up."

"How long have I been asleep?"

"Three hours."

Nat gulped. "Have the robots found anyone?"

Wen shook her head. "They've made one thousand and thirty-one calls. Nothing. But I've got another idea."

Nat swung her legs off the bed. "I need a Popko juice."

"We should start a search for Doctor Fairlight in Borneo. Mum did say that if anyone could find an antidote it'd be Fred," said Wen.

In the kitchen Nat found Fizz with his eyes half closed. His snout was flashing a dull orange. She took a large swig of cold Popko juice, fished out a cable from her pack and plugged him in. *Duh-duh-duh-duh-duh*. He whirred into life. His eyes opened as Nat typed in her search and a list of multi-layered links scrolled up on his screen. Feeling a burst of energy from the Popko juice she began to go through them. A colourful jungle logo caught her eye: *"Borneo's Governmental Department of the Environment."*

"If Doctor Fairlight was going on an expedition, I bet they'd know about it," she said. "Bintang Cho, Minister of the Environment, and here's his phone number. I'll need a voice masker as well as auto-translate."

Henry's eyes popped wide. "You've got a voice masker? Can I try it?"

Nat shook her head. She scrolled down the list of voices. "Let's try this," she said, selecting *"Headmistress"*.

She cleared her throat. "One, two, three, testing."

"ONE, TWO, THREE, TESTING!" repeated a

deep, booming lady's voice. Henry jumped in fright.

"*Ai yah!*" said Wen, wincing.

"Fizz, call Bintang Cho," said Nat.

A lady answered in a soft voice. "Good morning."

"May I please speak to Mr Bintang Cho," demanded Nat in her best Headmistress.

Henry and Wen started to giggle.

"Who may I say is calling?" said the lady.

"This is Nat Walker from Watchem Labs in Hong Kong. I have urgent business to discuss with Mr Cho."

"One moment, please."

A man answered.

"Minister, my name is Nat Walker and I'm calling on behalf of Watchem Labs in Hong Kong," said Nat, butterflies flapping in her stomach.

"Yes, Ms Walker, and what can I do for you?" replied the minister, his voice friendly.

"We need your help, sir. We have urgent information for Doctor Fred Fairlight. We understand she is on an expedition in Borneo."

"I haven't seen Doctor Fairlight for over three months," he replied.

Nat grinned. They had a lead. She gave the thumbs-up to the others.

"How can we contact her?"

"I issued Doctor Fairlight with a permit for an annual study of our native plants along the Sarawak river. She could be anywhere along it and I am sorry to say I have no contact details on file."

"It is most urgent that we find her. It is a matter of life and death."

There was a long pause before he replied.

"You could try Sarawak Tours. Doctor Fairlight travelled upriver with them."

Henry grabbed NutNut off the kitchen worktop. He paused the Borjigin search and looked up a Sarawak Tours brochure. A row of brightly coloured boats appeared on screen. A stocky man was standing on board grinning. He had a gold tooth, which glinted in the sun, and wore a white T-shirt with "Sarawak Tours" emblazoned in orange.

"Thank you, Minister. You have been most helpful," said Nat.

"I wish you good luck in your search," he said, and hung up.

Henry activated the brochure. Footage from a tour began; lots of smiling tourists sitting at the back of a boat as it ploughed through muddy water. Sounds of the jungle boomed out of NutNut's mouth.

"Call them!" said Wen.

A man answered.

"We took Doctor Fairlight to Nanga Gaat, long way upriver. Lot of baggage," he said after Nat had finished her introduction.

"Do you know where she is now?"

"She camps at old log camp, making experiments."

Henry found a map showing Nanga Gaat. Wen touched NutNut's screen to zoom in. It showed a thin strip of muddy river surrounded by thick forest.

"Can we contact her?"

The man noisily sucked in air and tut-tutted. "No phones. Delivery boat goes one time month. Need Fred you go by boat."

Nat hit the mute button and looked over at Wen. "What do we do?"

"Ask him how long it would take to get there," she said.

Nat's eyes widened.

"Hello? You there?" said the man.

Nat released the mute.

"If we come to Kuching, how long will it take to find Fred?" she asked.

"Two days. You want go? Take all credit cards."

Chapter Thirty
THE CALL

Supper in the Walker family kitchen was served by Ming. She was using bamboo tongs to fill Nat's bowl with a mound of greasy noodles.

"How was golf today?" said Aunt Vera frostily.

Uncle Fergal cleared his throat. "Good. Played a round with Xang Fu-Ping. Seems he's being transferred to London."

Aunt Vera arched one of her finely plucked brows. "He got a promotion too then."

There was no reply from the other end of the table. A heavy silence hung in the air. Prissy picked at her food. Henry ate quickly, checking his watch every few seconds and glancing nervously at Nat.

"Bennett, show Hong Kong NewsAmp, please," said Aunt Vera.

"*Yes, ma'am,*" said the house computer in the plummy tones of an English butler.

A reporter appeared on the Screenwall behind Nat's seat.

CRIMSON POISON

"Today's hottest amped-up news story comes out of Barzurka where it was reported today that a secret new weapon will be unveiled, which they claim will change world ord—"

"Call waiting from Doctor Tang for Mrs Walker," announced Bennett, pausing the news report.

Aunt Vera's chopsticks clattered on to the table. She jumped up and started fluffing her hair. Nat crossed her fingers under the table.

"Doctor Tang," said Aunt Vera. "What a most pleasant surprise."

Amplified through the surround speakers, Wen's mother's voice filled the room. "Mrs Walker, how kind of you to take my call. I trust all is well with you and your family?"

"Vera, please. Most well, and yours?"

"Very well, thank you, Vera. In fact, that's why I am calling. We're off to our beach house at Tai Long Wan tonight. I know it's very short notice but Wen would be so happy if Nat could join us. Jun left for extra study school in Shanghai yesterday. Wen misses his company and since it's only myself, my husband and Wen, I fear she might get bored. We would be most grateful if you would be so kind as to let Nat join us."

Aunt Vera looked like the cat that had got the yak

butter. Nat smiled. Wen had got the voice just right; she sounded just like her mother. Prissy was giving her dagger looks.

"Oh, Doctor Tang, goodness, what a kind invitation."

Nat looked over to see her aunt in deep thought. The silence was uncomfortable; she should have said something more. Uncle Fergal cleared his throat. Nat's heart missed a beat. What was Aunt Vera thinking?

"It might be a little difficult with Nat so…"

"I understand your concern but perhaps it might help if, once we've brought Nat back safe and sound, we arrange to have lunch at the Silver Dragon Club?"

Aunt Vera's face lit up. Nice work, Wen. Aunt Vera had never been to Hong Kong's most prestigious private members' club. An invite meant a big step up the social ladder.

"Indeed," she said. "We would be delighted to accept. Can I suggest that my daughter, Prissy, chaperone Nat…"

"What!" said Nat, jumping up from the table in fright.

Prissy scowled at her.

"I'm afraid not," said Doctor Tang aka Wen. "We only have room for one extra guest in our Speedcopter.

CRIMSON POISON

I do hope that won't stop Nat from joining us."

Nat sighed with relief. Thank goodness Wen was so quick.

"Oh, of course, I should have thought of that. Our friends the Wong-Xailais have the new generation Speedcopter FX 4. I forgot how compact they are." Aunt Vera forced a shrill hyena laugh.

Uncle Fergal harrumphed and raised a bushy eyebrow. Henry held his head in his hands, cringing at his mother's attempt to suck up to Doctor Tang.

"Wonderful, Vera. I'll take that as a yes. Wen will be delighted," said Wen. "I'll have our driver pick up Nat within the hour."

Chapter Thirty-One
ESCAPE

A stretch Grooverider glided up to the steps of Wetley Towers. A man in a white chauffeur's uniform stepped out of the driver's seat and walked round to the passenger door. Nat hoisted her backpack over her shoulder and tried to blink. She wasn't used to the thick mascara and eyeshadow that had been applied by Prissy under strict orders of Aunt Vera. Prissy had raked her hair into a topknot and sprayed it hard like concrete. Worst of all was the Schmancy neon suit with a silver trim that felt like a straitjacket.

"Now," said Aunt Vera. "Mind your manners. We don't want to let the side down, do we?"

Nat forced a smile. "No," she said.

Aunt Vera leaned in and pecked her on both cheeks.

"I'll take Nat to the car, Mummy," said Henry, taking Nat's hand.

"How kind, Henry," said Aunt Vera with a smile.

The chauffeur took Nat's backpack as she slid into the back seat of the Grooverider.

CRIMSON POISON

"*Ai yah*, Nat! What has the witch done to you?" squealed Wen, giving her a hug. "A typhoon couldn't destroy that hairstyle."

"I wish I could come too," moaned Henry, sticking his head inside the car. "Wow, this is as big as my bedroom!"

"You're needed here, Henry," said Nat. "Remember. You're back-up."

Henry's cheeks began to burn. "*Ku!*"

"We're counting on you," said Nat, squeezing his hand. "We couldn't do this without you."

"Hurry up, Henry," called Aunt Vera, tapping her stiletto on the marble steps.

"Got to go, good luck!" he said.

The door closed and the Grooverider moved off. Nat leaned back into the deep leather seat.

"You should check out what's in my backpack. Aunt Vera stuffed it with a whole Schmancy wardrobe," she said, trying to shake out her hair; it wouldn't budge. She raked her fingers through it, but the hair stayed stiffly in place.

"Agh!" she cried in frustration, kicking off her pink wedges. "I just want to be me again."

"And so you shall," said Wen, waving her finger like a magic wand. "I took the liberty of…" She produced a blue bag and handed it to Nat.

"Thanks, Wen!" said Nat, pulling out a Tiger Rocks Out T-shirt, a pair of Slider shorts and Trenko sneakers.

"I nearly bought you some Mito jeans but I knew you'd never wear them."

"Lucky Movie Theatre, Miss Wen," announced the driver, pulling up outside the main doors.

Wen climbed out. "Thank you, Shin."

"Enjoy the film," said the driver with a short bow. "Do you need me to take you both back to Wetley Towers later?"

"No, we'll make our own way back, thank you."

Throngs of people were heading into the cinema. The Grooverider pulled away. Wen grabbed Nat's arm and steered her off down the street.

"We've got to hurry, we've only got two hours to get the plane."

Chapter Thirty-Two
BORNEO BOUND

"Natalie Walker and Wen Tang, please follow me," said the flight attendant in a Tiger Airlines orange-and-black-striped catsuit.

Sitting in the seats marked "Special Services" in the departure lounge, Nat and Wen stood up and followed the flight attendant, trying not to fiddle with their plastic "Unaccompanied Minor" badges.

The flight attendant led them on to the plane, seating them in Row A before the rest of the passengers arrived.

"I hope we get Coco-Zaps as the snack," said Wen, kicking off her sandals.

"I'm too nervous to eat," said Nat.

"We'll be back before anyone realises we're gone," said Wen, pushing the airline pillow behind her head. "I'm meant to be staying at the witch's Wetley lair, and you're with me at the beach house. Your aunt is too busy thinking about the Dragon Club invitation and my mum is too busy with a new deadline at work.

You've got to admit, it's the perfect plan!"

"*Zoinks*, I hope so," said Nat, closing her eyes.

"We're going on an adventure. Let's enjoy the ride," said Wen, putting on her eyeshade.

The other passengers began to board. Nat started to bite her nails.

"Wen," she said, giving her a nudge. "What's the name of the man who's meeting us again?"

"Ikat Santang."

"Even with the voice modifier do you really think he believed that I was a grown-up?"

Wen lifted her eyeshade. "*Ai yah*, you worry too much!"

Nat nodded. Wen was right. She tried to close her eyes but big, uneasy questions played in her head. *Would they find Doctor Fairlight? Was Jamuka still alive? Would they get found out?*

"Play sailing movie fifteen, Fizz," she said, needing some kind of distraction.

His eyes fluttered open and he spread his wings. Jamuka appeared on screen at the wheel of the *Junko*. Nat stood next to him. She was three years old. Her tiny hand was holding his as he showed her how to steer the boat with the wind.

She watched herself – so serious one moment,

giggling the next – as Jamuka scooped her up in his arms. She wished she could turn back the clock.

Three hours later the plane landed in Kuching. A Tiger Airlines escort led them through customs to arrivals, where a crowd of tour operators were gathered.

"That's us," said Nat, spotting a man holding up a wooden board with their names scrawled in black ink. She waved, catching the man's eye. He smiled and hurried over. He was no taller than they were, and wore a white T-shirt with *"Johnson's Engines"* written on the front. Instead of shorts he was dressed in a long sarong.

"I am Ikat Santang," he said with a big toothy grin. "Welcome to Kuching."

The airline escort handed them over. Ikat shook their hands vigorously, pumping them up and down.

"Follow me," he said, with a wave towards the exit.

They stepped outside. The humidity hit Nat like a wet towel. They passed a line of taxis and arrived at a white minibus with *"Sarawak Tours"* painted down the side.

A policeman marched across the road, blowing his whistle.

"In quick!" urged Ikat, opening the door.

They jumped inside. Ikat slammed the door shut and started the engine, ignoring the policeman, who by now was banging on the driver's window and shouting. He threw the minibus into gear and pulled away.

Nat looked at Wen in alarm. An icy draught of air conditioning blasted through the van, making her shiver. They left the airport and sped out on to the main road. Ikat pressed down hard on the accelerator. Metal chimes jangled noisily from the mirror.

"We go to boat," he shouted over a Malaysian pop song blaring on the radio.

"How far?" asked Nat, gripping the door handle.

"Ten minutes. Boat ready. We go."

Ikat dropped a gear, rammed his foot down hard to coax more speed from the old minibus and pulled out to overtake a slow-moving car in front. Just as they drew alongside, a pair of bright headlights came into view, hurtling straight towards them. Nat closed her eyes.

"*Ai yah!*" cried Wen.

Ikat swerved just in time to avoid the oncoming car. The angry driver beeped his horn.

Fizz started snorting, smoke billowing out of his nostrils. Fu let out a high-pitched squeal.

CRIMSON POISON

"Cool fire dragon!" shouted Ikat, glancing at them through the rear-view mirror.

"He's a worse driver than Granny Tang," said Wen.

Nat clutched Fizz close. She looked out of the window to see brightly painted shopfronts locked up for the night with metal shutters. A pack of dogs was on the loose, nosing through rubbish bins, on the hunt for supper. Small knots of people were milling around, but otherwise the city was asleep. It was a ghost town compared to Hong Kong.

Ten minutes later Ikat came screeching to a halt at the edge of a rickety wooden pier. A blinking sign read Tunku Jetty. A row of longboats, sitting low in the water, roped to their moorings, bobbed up and down. One of the boats had a spotlight on its roof while the others floated in darkness. A man was standing on its roof.

"Peja!" shouted Ikat. The man looked up and waved.

"Road stop, river start," said Ikat, helping them out of the minibus. "You good sailors?"

"Yes, I live on a boat," said Nat.

He threw back his head and laughed.

Nat had no idea what was so funny. "Will we be safe?"

"Never lost passenger. Sarawak Tours first class."
He held up his right hand, which was missing a finger.
"Five-star safety rating. You in safe hands."

Nat was relieved to see two enormous engines strapped to the stern as she stepped into the small cockpit. Peja greeted them with a bow and the same toothy grin as Ikat. He led them down the stairs into the cabin.

"*Ai yah*, this is so last century," said Wen.

The cabin was lit up like a Christmas tree with multicoloured fairy lights. Flowered curtains covered the windows, and rows of Hong Kong Air seats were bolted to the floor, leaving enough room for a narrow walkway down the middle. At the front, hanging off a steel rail, was an old TV. All the seats, except for two at the back, were piled high with boxes, bags and pallets of fizzy drinks. A loud *cluck-cluck* came from some crates. It was followed by a hiss.

"Sounds like a travelling zoo," said Nat, lifting up a metal cage containing three chickens and a cockerel. "What's all this stuff for?"

"People upriver," said Peja on his way back to the cockpit. "You stay here. Dangerous river."

Nat jumped as the engines roared into action, sending vibrations through the boat. She climbed into the seat next to the window and pulled back the curtain.

"Fizz. Film," she said, holding him up.

The boat was already reversing off its mooring.

The TV crackled into life. A grainy Chinese gangster movie started to play at full volume. The fairy lights began to flash on and off.

"Isn't first-class travel..." Wen stopped and wrinkled her nose. "Can you smell that?"

Nat sniffed the air. "*Zoinks!*"

She put Fizz on the window ledge, stepped across Wen's seat and made her way up to the front row of seats as the boat jolted through the water.

She peered into a wooden crate.

"Aha, the king of fruits!" she said, pulling out a large green spiky fruit.

"Yuk. Durian is not the king, it's the stinker of fruits," said Wen.

"The smelly sock stinker of fruits," said Nat, putting it back.

She returned to her seat.

"Time for some *zzzzzzs*," said Wen, pulling on her eyeshade again.

Nat couldn't sleep. The word *poison* was swimming around in her mind like a menacing, circling shark.

"Search NewsAmp, Fizz. Looking for new poison or sickness reports in Mongolia," she whispered.

He turned his snout so that it was now close to her ear. "*No news found,*" he whispered.

She sighed with relief. "Show me the top news story."

Fizz spread his wings. A text-based report showed on screen: "*Rumours abound about the undisclosed Barzurkan mega-weapon. General Golkova remains tight-lipped on details.*"

Chapter Thirty-Three
TRICKY BUSINESS

He examined the diagram one more time, double-checking the incision point, before pulling the scalpel carefully out of its pouch. The fine silver blade glinted in the overhead light. Taking a deep breath, he put his good eye to the microscope. A droplet of sweat fell on to the eyepiece. He wiped it away with his sleeve and tried again. This time the petal came into sharp focus, blood red, the electric blue like a neon strip.

He brought the scalpel under the microscope and positioned it so that the tip of the blade was at the top, where the blue and red met. His hand trembled and he nearly scored the petal. This was harder than he thought. All the bravado he had mustered to report to the Barzurkan General about his progress had vanished the moment he had left the tent.

He took another deep breath and exhaled slowly before repositioning the blade. The veins in the petal were easily visible. All he had to do was draw a line with the scalpel between the major third and fourth ones, making sure he only severed a maximum of eight of the spider veins, which ran between them.

The blade sliced through two spider veins. He continued to cut, trying to trace around the others but it was useless.

"*Ugui!*" he said, watching the petal begin to curl, the beautiful red and blue fading to brown.

It folded in on itself, withering before his eyes. His priceless weapon had once again turned into dust.

Chapter Thirty-Four
TROUBLE ON THE RIVER

Nat woke to the rattle of machine-gun fire on the television. Daylight filtered through the net curtain. She felt stiff and cold from the icy air conditioning.

"Fizz, where are you?" she said, her teeth chattering.

"*Window, recharging,*" came his robotic voice from behind the curtain.

She reached underneath and picked him up off the ledge.

"Messages?"

"*One from Henry.*"

"Show me."

Fizz opened his wings. Henry appeared on screen. He was in his bedroom, still in his pyjamas.

"*Hai*, Nat. Did you get to Borneo? Mummy just came in and told me to put on my suit. We're going to her lawyers about you. I'll try to record it. I miss you. *Bai*," he said.

Nat swallowed hard. The guardianship – Aunt Vera really was going to fight for it. She closed her eyes, wishing for Jamuka to come back safe and sound.

She stepped over Wen, who was sound asleep under a sarong, and headed for the deck. It was like climbing out of a freezer into an oven.

Ikat waved from the helm. Nat smiled, waving back. The air was filled with the roar of the engines propelling the boat up a muddy brown river at high speed. On either side dense jungle gave off a rich, musky odour. Nat grabbed on to the side rail to keep her balance. The sun shone down from a clear sky. Happiness unexpectedly bubbled up inside her – it was good to be on deck again.

Looking upriver she saw a big tree trunk floating towards them. She braced herself for the bump but the boat's steel nose just pushed it out of the way.

"Logging camps," shouted Ikat. "Dump trees in river. Free transport!"

Nat smiled.

As the sun reached higher, the river began to narrow. Ikat slowed the engines. Birdsong and buzzing insects replaced the engine roar. Nat ate the last of the coconut rice Peja had given her, kicked off her shoes and dangled her feet over the side. Cool water splashed up her legs as she gazed out at rainforest.

CRIMSON POISON

Soaring trees with leaves as big as plates reached out across the water.

A sudden yell in the distance broke the calm, followed by a chorus of angry shouts. The pointed nose of a canoe came racing round the bend up ahead. Someone was paddling towards them at a furious pace. Nat shaded her eyes and squinted against the sunlight bouncing off the water. A figure dressed in khaki, wearing a wide-brimmed hat, was sitting in front of a stack of crates, weighing the canoe dangerously low in the water.

Ikat cut the boat's engines.

She saw another canoe come round the bend in hot pursuit. Two men wearing bandanas round their heads, black vests and camouflage trousers were paddling at a clip. Nat gasped. One of them stood up and waved a machete in the air, its blade glinting menacingly in the sun.

"Pirates. Go inside!" said Ikat, opening the hatch as Peja ran across the roof with a metal anchor on a rope.

Nat sprang down the steps. The hatch slammed shut behind her.

"*Hai*, Nat!" said Wen. "I just got a message about those discounted *ding* Mito jeans—"

Nat grabbed Wen's arm, her eyes wide with fear.

"Pirates," she gasped. "Outside. They've got a machete."

Wen laughed. "Ha! You've been watching too much bad TV."

Nat leaned across to pull back the curtain.

"Real pirates, Wen. Look!"

They peered through the grubby window. The pirates were nearly at the boat. There was a loud thud. Shouts erupted like gunfire.

Wen's hand flew to her mouth. "*Ai yah!*"

"They're chasing another canoe full of crates," said Nat.

There was another thud on the roof, followed by heavy footsteps. The pirate with the machete was now waving it from side to side.

Wen shrieked as an anchor came flying across the water, knocking the pirate off his feet.

"*Zoinks!*" said Nat. "One down."

The other pirate lunged towards the boat, leaping on board. The first pirate's hand slapped against Nat and Wen's window as he pulled himself up, out of the river.

"*Ai yah!*" cried Wen. "They're coming on board."

More heavy thuds hit the roof. An ear-piercing scream sounded out.

CRIMSON POISON

Fizz's eyes lit up bright red. Thick smoke came billowing out of his snout. Fu started thumping her feet in alarm.

"Stop!" said Wen, clamping her hand over Fu. "You'll give us away."

Peja's face flew past the window. He splashed into the river.

"Oh, no! That leaves Ikat against two pirates," said Nat, her mind spinning. "There's only one thing for it. We're going to have to take action."

"We can hide under our seats," said Wen.

"But they'll find us. I mean real action," said Nat, her eyes scanning the cabin.

Wen frowned. "What? You mean, real action, *gun fu* stuff, just like Scowler Stone?"

Nat nodded, jumping into the gangway and making her way to the front.

"Are you mad? They're big, we're kids and this is real. It's not the movies."

Nat reached over and picked up a cage. The cockerels inside began squawking. Fizz blew smoke at them, making them squawk even more.

"Stop, Fizz! We can use these," she said, holding it up.

Wen screwed up her face. "You think you're going

to beat two pirates armed with machetes with two cockerels? They'll chop them up and have them for supper."

Nat ignored her, ran over to another seat, dragged a heavy box on to the floor and pushed it up towards the hatch.

"And for your next trick?" said Wen.

Nat opened the box.

"No way!" said Wen.

"If we don't do anything the pirates will get us and I hate to think what they might do with us. So, take your pick."

Nat pointed inside the box with one hand and held out the cage in the other.

Wen took the cage.

"Right. This is my plan," said Nat.

Chapter Thirty-Five
FRED

Two minutes later Nat undid the bolt and yanked open the hatch. Outside in the cockpit Ikat was engaged in a fierce battle with one of the pirates, using a metal pole to fend off the thrusts of the machete.

"One, two, three," whispered Nat.

The pirate spun round just as Nat and Wen jumped up, each holding a cockerel. They hurled the cockerels at the pirate. The birds opened their wings in fright, hitting him squarely in the face.

"Argh!" he cried, dropping the machete.

Wasting no time, Ikat hit him hard with the pole. He fell to the ground, out cold, the two bewildered cockerels landing on top of him.

"*Ding!*" shouted Wen, punching the air.

Nat spun round to see the other pirate up on the roof. He was wrestling with the giant canoeist who was clutching a crate.

Nat jumped up.

"Here," said Wen, passing her the box.

Nat set it down on the roof and reached in for a spiky durian fruit about the size of a football. She aimed at the pirate and threw it as hard as she could. He saw it and ducked but Nat had already picked up a smaller one. This time the fruit hit his arm, exploding on contact.

The pirate roared, let go of the crate and charged at Nat. The third durian hit him on the shoulder, but it didn't stop him. Nat crouched down.

This was for real. This wasn't just another sparring session with Jamuka. As the pirate launched himself at her, she rolled to one side, leapt up and kicked him as hard as she could in the stomach.

With a loud grunt, the pirate lost his footing and went flying off the roof into the river below.

"Bravo, young lady," sang the giant canoeist.

Nat gasped. "You're a woman!"

Ikat revved the boat's engines. He thrust them into reverse, getting as much distance between them and the pirate in the water as possible. Nat flew backwards, landing in the cockpit on a sopping-wet Peja, who had managed to clamber back on board.

"You are one kung fu jade babe. Ken would be proud," said Wen, giving her a hand up.

"Good work!" shouted Ikat with a grin.

Nat smiled with relief. Her heart was hammering in her chest. It had been a close call.

"Arrest that man!" sang the enormous woman, hitting a top note.

She was standing on the roof, looking down into the cockpit, clutching her crate and pointing at the other pirate, who Peja had bound and gagged. "You snivelling orchid thief! He nearly got his hands on my *Semper lucidias*."

"Doctor Fairlight," said Ikat, nodding. "Trouble again."

"You're Doctor Fred Fairlight?" said Nat, taking in the bright-red cheeks under a shaggy mop of grey hair, and a pair of thick pebble glasses perched on the end of a big, knobbly nose.

Fred clambered off the roof. She towered over them like a big bear.

"Indeed I am. Very good to meet you," she said, pumping Nat's hand up and down. "Just call me Fred, please."

"I'm Natalie Walker and this is my friend Wen Tang."

"I'm Doctor Tang's daughter," said Wen.

Fred's bushy eyebrows shot up in surprise. "Amazing. How is your mother?"

"Very well. She sent us to find you."

Fred lifted the top off the crate and produced a tall, spindly green plant with several jet-black flowers. "This is the most splendid specimen of *Semper lucidias* known to exist. Most exciting. I had to climb to the top of a tree to get it." She lifted it up to the sky. "Up, up to the to-o-p…" she sang, scaling an octave.

Nat glanced over at Wen.

Wen winked. "Mad as a snake," she whispered.

"Doctor Fairlight, we go Kuching?" said Ikat.

"Kuching? Goodness me, no, I must get back to my camp. Drop me off downriver at Nanga Gaat longhouse, please. But take that rascal," she pointed to the pirate, "to the police station in Kuching. I'll give you a written note for the police commissioner."

"No," said Nat. "Please, you must come to Kuching. Like Wen said, Doctor Tang told us to come and find you. You're the only one who can help save the Clan."

Fred looked up and blinked.

"Save the Clan?"

"In Mongolia," said Wen.

"Tumen Vachir," said Nat. "Have you ever heard of Marbolic?"

Fred let out a loud snort.

CRIMSON POISON

"Of course I know about Marbolic. It's a terrible poison made from a fertiliser called Growemup. I told them before they had completed trials that the product was going to start an environmental disaster. Is that what's happened?"

Between them Nat and Wen told Fred everything they knew while Ikat drove the boat downriver.

"Nanga Gaat longhouse," he announced, pulling into a low wooden dock on the far bank.

Fred picked up her crate. "What a right old mess you've found yourselves in. I suggest you call the Mongolian army. It's their job to clean up this sort of thing."

"But Mum said if anyone could find the antidote, it's you," said Wen.

Fred nodded. "The problem is I'm extremely busy with my orchid studies. I'm on a very tight deadline to hand in my paper and I've still got several major experiments to conduct."

"You've got to help save the Clan. Without an antidote they'll die," said Nat, no longer caring if she sounded panicked. "Please."

Peja jumped on to the dock with the mooring rope.

"Quite impossible," said Fred, packing away the orchid. "I'll lose all my funding if I don't complete my studies. As I said, try the army. They should be able to find out who's using Growemup and put a stop to it. Now, if you'll excuse me…"

She stepped out on to the dock.

"How much funding will you get?" asked Wen.

"One hundred thousand US dollars," said Fred.

"We'll double it," said Wen. "Triple it!"

Fred turned and blinked. "Look, girls, you couldn't possibly come up with such a princely sum…"

"Have you heard of SPIN?" said Nat.

"Who?" said Fred.

"The Walker games company," said Ikat, cutting the engines.

Nat nodded.

Wen held up three fingers. "*Empire of the Shadow, Wand of Truth* and *Lavanter*. Come on. You must have heard of SPIN's top-three world-number-one games!"

Fred snorted. "That's bounty indeed but your parents might not want to part with their hard-earned cash."

Nat bit her lip. "They're dead."

"She's an orphan," said Wen.

Fred peered at Nat, her head cocked to one side.

"You're serious about this, aren't you?"

CRIMSON POISON

"Very." Nat nodded.

They stood in silence for a moment, the squawks and hum of the jungle closing in.

"Well, Miss Walker." Fred's mouth opened into a strange lopsided smile as if she was sucking a toffee. She headed back towards the boat. "What are we waiting for?"

Chapter Thirty-Six
CUSTODY

The Walkers were sitting in the kitchen slurping crab and noodle soup for supper. Prissy was in a sulk. She stirred her spoon noisily while across the table Henry stared into his bowl, his food untouched. He glanced anxiously at NutNut. His squirrel hadn't made a sound since he'd sent Nat the video, and that was over three hours ago.

"Prissy, stop that," snapped Aunt Vera, reaching across and snatching away Prissy's spoon.

"It tastes disgusting," said Prissy.

"Go to your room!" Aunt Vera pointed towards the door.

Prissy scraped her chair back slowly on the marble floor. Everybody winced. She grabbed her glitter cat robot off the table, stood up, turned on her high-heeled mules and clacked out of the room, slamming the door behind her.

Silence fell.

Uncle Fergal picked up his crystal tumbler and

took a swig of whisky. "Got ourselves a real teenager, haven't we?"

Vera pursed her lips. "I said she couldn't have Candy over for a sleepover. The Brat is back tomorrow."

Henry squeezed NutNut's right ear to trigger his recording function. NutNut's ears twitched.

Uncle Fergal nodded. "Did the papers arrive from the lawyer?"

Vera turned and picked up a large brown envelope from the shelf behind her. A sly smile spread across her lips.

"You'll never have to work again." She wafted the envelope tantalisingly beneath his nose.

Henry felt sick as he watched his father pull out a thick sheaf of typed white papers from the envelope.

"I have to hand it to you, Vera, you've pulled a rabbit out of a hat," he said, flicking through them.

"It wasn't easy. The only loophole we could find was to file for 'abandonment by guardian'. Ah Wong has acted as witness to say that Jamuka abandoned Natalie without due care. It cost a bit, she's a smart woman and she asked for a lot of money. I've told her I'll pay her when we get guardianship and access to the SPIN fortune. I see it as a worthwhile expense."

"And when do we get custody?"

"Jamuka isn't here to fight our claim. Since we're claiming it's abandonment we only have to legally wait a week." Vera clapped her hands together. "We're going to be richer than we ever dreamed of."

"And the Brat?"

"I've already spoken with the estate agent and briefed him to find us a house on the Peak. It must have a wing where she can be kept separately with an adjoining nanny's room."

Uncle Fergal nodded in agreement. "Very wise. We don't want her becoming part of the family, do we?"

Henry felt like punching him. How could they be so greedy and horrible? Instead he bit his tongue and looked down at his bowl. He coughed loudly and made a spluttering sound.

"Not feeling too bright, eh, Henry?" said his father.

Henry slumped his shoulders and shook his head.

"We'd better get the boy to bed, Vera. He's not touched his supper."

Vera looked startled, as though she had forgotten that her son was at the table.

"Go to bed, Henry darling. We need you back on your feet to go house-hunting tomorrow, bright and early."

Henry stood up from his chair and walked limply

towards the door, leaving NutNut on the table, still recording.

"Darling, have you forgotten your manners?" called out Aunt Vera.

He looked up to see her pointing at her cheek. He felt as if he were kissing a poisonous snake.

Chapter Thirty-Seven
ALTAN

"*Ai yah*, the witch!" said Wen, when Henry's recording had finished playing.

Tears streamed down Nat's cheeks. How could Aunt Vera and Uncle Fergal be so cold and calculating?

Fizz leaned his head against her shoulder at the sound of her sniffing.

"We'll find a way to stop them," said Wen, offering her a tissue.

"In a week?" said Nat. "We don't even know how to find Jamuka."

"*Call from Henry,*" said Fizz.

"Take it," said Nat.

He opened his wings to reveal Henry in his bedroom.

"I'm really sorry, Nat," he said. "Mummy and Daddy are vile."

Nat tried to smile as she wiped away her tears with the back of her hand.

"We'd better find Jamuka fast and stop them," said Wen.

Henry nodded. "NutNut's still searching for Borjigins but none of them come from the Clan."

"Keep looking. We are too," said Wen.

"Where are you?" said Henry.

"With Doctor Fairlight," said Nat.

She angled Fizz to focus on Fred, who was reclining in her seat, fast asleep, snoring with her mouth wide open, exposing a row of higgledy-piggledy yellow teeth.

"She looks scary."

"Mad as a hatter," said Nat, back on screen. "But she knows all about Tumen Vachir and Marbolic, and we've got her to agree to come to Mongolia."

"*Ku!*"

"But unless we find someone who knows where the Clan is, we're stuck," said Wen.

Henry leaned into camera. "I have to go. Mummy's calling," he whispered. "*Bai.*"

The screen went black.

"We'd better see how the robots are getting on then," said Nat.

Fizz and Fu had contacted thousands of Borjigins, but with no luck. Wen was now fast asleep with Fu curled up on her lap. Fu's nose was still twitching as she continued to search. Nat peeped under the curtain. It was pitch black outside as the boat slid past the riverbank. Before long they would be back in Kuching. How could they send Fred to Mongolia if they didn't know how to find the Clan?

She rubbed her eyes.

"Fizz, call Jamuka."

"*Out of range. Leave message?*"

"No, show Borjigin list."

He opened his wings. She must have tried over a hundred times to reach Jamuka. *What if he had been poisoned too?* That was a question that ran through her head on a constant loop.

The endless list appeared on screen. She started to scroll down it. A flashing advertisement at the side of the screen caught her attention:

Taban Boarding School. A private educational institution in the heart of Ulan Bator, providing a home away from home for children of the Steppe.

If there weren't any schools in the mountains, perhaps the Clan kids had to go to the city to learn? It was worth a try.

"Activate auto-translate and voice mask, Fizz. Use

'old man' voice modifier."

His eyes flashed amber.

"Call Taban Boarding School, voice only."

Fizz lowered his wings.

"Hello, Taban Boarding School," answered a woman's voice.

"Hello. My name is Jamuka Borjigin. I'm calling from the Hentii Mountains with an urgent message for all the students from our family in the region."

There was a pause.

"One moment, please."

Nat was put on hold. Her heartbeat quickened. She rehearsed what she should say next. The minutes ticked by. She wondered if she'd been forgotten when a boy's voice came on the line. *"Hello. I am Altan Borjigin, son of Tabin."*

Tabin? That sounded like a familiar name. She was sure Jamuka had mentioned him before. She switched off the voice modifier.

"Hai. This is Nat Walker. Listen, I'm a friend of Jamuka Borjigin."

"Jamuka? He is my uncle. Is he OK?"

"The Clan and the wolves are very sick," explained Nat. "Jamuka has gone to the Hentii Mountains to help them."

She shook Wen awake.

"What's up?" said Wen, bleary eyed.

Nat held her finger to her lips. She told Altan everything she knew.

"*I must go to the Clan,*" said Altan, the panic rising in his voice.

"You have to meet Doctor Fairlight at the airport and take her with you. I will book it now and call you right back."

She ended the call.

"Not so fast," sang out Fred, leaning across the aisle. "This expedition needs assistants and that's you." She jabbed a finger at Nat and Wen.

"But we have to get back to Hong Kong," said Nat.

Fred shook her head. "That won't do at all. You're essential to the success of this mission. Besides, it's bad luck to change crew midstream."

"*Ai yah!* That's impossible. My parents will lock me away for the rest of my life. I'll never shop again, I'll never see daylight…" said Wen.

Fred folded her arms across her chest. "You came to find me. Now I need you to help me solve the case."

Nat's mind was racing with possibilities. "If I go to Mongolia with Doctor Fairlight, I can find Jamuka and make him realise he has to come back in time to stop Aunt Vera."

"I can tell the witch you're staying on with us," said Wen. "Our plan worked last time."

Nat looked at her best friend. "You would?"

Wen took Nat's hand and squeezed it. "I'll cover for you."

Fred snorted. "Well, I suppose one assistant is better than none."

Chapter Thirty-Eight
ELIXIR

He closed the door. Kicking the snow off his boots, he walked over to the metal table and sat down. The walk uphill had left him breathless. Ever since the wind had started to gust, everything had become harder. The guards had spent the afternoon battening down the greenhouses while he had been inside checking the plants. If only the General had given him more time, they could have done all this in the summer when the conditions were ideal, not in the harsh winter when they had to battle to keep the heat and light working to make sure the plants bloomed.

He opened the bag and brought out two petals. One was large, the other small. It was the entire day's harvest from the crop. Before he placed the first one under the microscope, he grabbed his bottle of *airag* and took a swig. The strong, sour fermented horse milk burned the back of his throat and its fire spread through his body. Two more chances to get it right.

CRIMSON POISON

Two more days until the General came back. Results were expected if he wanted to get his money.

The scalpel severed five spider veins. One more and he was nearly there, the pattern complete. Just as he was about to twist the blade around another vein, the door was flung open, letting in an icy blast of air. The blade slipped, tearing through the petal.

"*Ugui!*" he said, watching it wither and die.

He threw the scalpel across the table.

"General come tomorrow," said the guard, standing in the doorway. "Be ready test weapon."

Before he could reply, the guard slammed the door and disappeared.

Tomorrow?

He was meant to have another day. He took another swig of *airag* before picking up the last, small petal and placing it under the microscope. It took a few moments to focus right. Then he saw what he had been waiting for – a petal with only six spider veins.

He retrieved the scalpel, made the incision and drew a line straight down the petal. It split into two and from the split oozed a deep-red blood-like liquid. As he watched it spill across the glass slide, an evil, satisfied smile spread across his face.

Chapter Thirty-Nine
HOUSE-HUNTING

Aunt Vera was sitting in the sunroom sipping jasmine tea.

"Oh, just listen to this, Henry," she said, patting her son's hand.

The brochures from the estate agent had arrived and his mother was excitedly scanning through the luxury properties. Henry had little choice but to listen. He was under strict orders to get some light therapy in the sunroom. With no time to protest he had been frogmarched in his striped blue pyjamas and tucked up in a scratchy tartan rug on the sofa.

Sunlight spilled through the window, reflecting off the gilt-framed mirrors on the wall. Fake Ming vases stood on spindly tables. A silk rug covered the floor, on which stood fake pieces of Louis XIV furniture. Henry squinted, wishing he could go back to his dark cave of a bedroom – or better still be with Nat and Doctor Fairlight on their way to Mongolia.

"A majestic villa of historic significance nestled in

its own private gardens on the Peak," read Aunt Vera, her horn-rimmed reading glasses perched on the tip of her nose. "Sounds perfect."

She thrust her FastPad on to Henry's lap. The house looked like a palace. "But we're fine here, Mummy," he said. "We don't need to move."

Aunt Vera took his hand and squeezed it. "My little darling. It's not a case of need, it's a case of deserve." She jabbed at the photograph with a bony finger.

"*Incoming postcard from Doctor Tang for Mrs Walker,*" announced Bennett.

Aunt Vera sprang to attention. "Open it."

The shutters automatically half lowered over the windows as the room's Screenwall activated. Henry's heart started to race. This was it. The background image of the beach he had spent hours perfecting appeared. Nat and Wen were sitting side by side in matching spotty swimsuits, their faces hidden behind sunglasses, holding tall ice-cream sundae glasses.

"Hello, Aunt Vera. I just want you to know that I'm having the best time of my life here with Wen," said Nat, waving into camera. "We've been swimming and now we're having blueberry-butterscotch-banana ice-cream sundaes."

Henry smiled. His work looked good. Actually, not

just good, but amazing.

"I've been invited to stay for another week. I didn't think you'd mind, so I've said yes. Bye-bye, Aunt Vera. Send my love to Prissy."

"Hang on," said Aunt Vera as Nat's face faded from view. "Now, I'm not sure about that."

Henry grabbed his mother's hand and put on his angelic face.

"But, Mummy, a week's not long. And it's so nice being here on our own."

Aunt Vera ruffled his hair. "My poor darling, is the Brat very hard to live with?"

Henry bit his tongue. He hated having to lie.

"Yes, Mummy. I much prefer it when it's just us," he said, clutching on to NutNut's furry tail.

Aunt Vera smiled. "I like the way you think, Master Henry Walker. You are your mother's son. Let's get the house purchase underway before she returns."

Chapter Forty
AN ICY ARRIVAL

"Excuse me," said a flight attendant, touching Nat's shoulder. "Would you like a snack before we land?"

Nat lifted her eye mask.

"Yes, please," she said with a cavernous yawn.

The flight attendant placed a tray on her lap. Nat looked down to find a limp-looking sandwich and a small container of orange juice, which she opened and gratefully swigged. Lifting the top slice of bread revealed a piece of hard yellow cheese. Yuk.

Across the aisle, Fred was snoring loudly, her hat resting over her face. A large handwritten sign reading *Do not disturb me under ANY circumstances* had been taped to her hat.

Nat leaned across. "Fred. We're about to land."

The snoring stopped, the hat lifted. Fred grabbed the sandwich from Nat's outstretched hand and took a big bite.

"Sustenance for the mission ahead," she said, chewing fast.

The plane's engines slowed and the "*Fasten Seatbelt*" sign lit up.

"Prepare for landing," announced the captain.

High winds buffeted the plane as it started its descent. When the wheels bumped down, they skidded across the icy runway. Nat gripped the arms of her seat as the plane juddered and the tyres screeched. She was pleased she'd put Fizz in plane mode otherwise he'd be blowing smoke and snorting like a crazed wild boar.

The plane came to an abrupt halt. The other passengers broke into a flurry of activity, leaping up out of their seats, opening the overhead lockers, pulling out thick coats, hats and gloves, and racing to put them on.

A woman reached into the locker above Nat's head and pulled out a grey fur hat. She glanced down at Nat in her shorts and T-shirt and shook her head, tutting, before making her way back to her seat.

"I suspect she thinks we're ill-dressed for a blizzard," said Fred.

Stepping on to the jetway, Nat was hit by a wall of the most intense cold she had ever experienced while Fred strode out in her khaki shirt and shorts as if she was still in the jungle.

CRIMSON POISON

"Those flight attendants were most unhelpful. Firstly, I missed my breakfast. Secondly, I could do with another one of those sandwiches. I'm going to file a complaint," she said.

Nat's teeth were chattering too hard to reply.

"Come on," said Fred, pushing her way to the front of the line for passport control. Nat followed, averting her eyes from the furious glances of the other passengers.

"Purpose?" said the official, raising an eyebrow.

"Science," said Fred. "We are here on an expedition of the utmost importance. I am Doctor Fairlight, PPDED, honorary member of the Royal Society of Botanists, and this is my trusted assistant, Miss Natalie Walker."

She thrust their passports under his nose.

The official examined the passports, the stamps and visas.

"Welcome to Mongolia. I hope you will find warmer clothes for your expedition," he said with a smile.

They hauled Fred's crates off a creaky old luggage belt on to a rusty trolley and exited into the arrivals area. Nat looked at the sea of faces. Everyone was staring at them, nudging each other, pointing and laughing.

A tall boy dressed in a long blue coat and fur hat pushed through the crowds, a large bag swinging from his shoulder. He could only have been a few years older than Nat and had high cheekbones with bright, rosy cheeks.

"*Tavtai morilogtun*. I am Altan Borjigin," he said with a short bow. "You easy to spot."

"An ab-so-luu-uute plea-sss-uuure," sang Fred, shaking his hand vigorously.

"You singer?" he said, his brow furrowing.

"Doctor Fairlight's the name and, yes, I'm partial to a bit of opera," she said, her words scaling an arpeggio. "I was once fortunate enough to understudy in *Carmen*. A libretto—"

"You Mat?" He turned to Nat.

"Nat."

"Sorry," he said, looking at her boyish clothes with a grin. "Hard to tell."

She scowled. He dumped the bag on the floor and unzipped the top. Out burst an explosion of fur coats.

"Looks like you raided the local zoo," said Nat.

Altan reached in and pulled out hats, coats, trousers, socks and shirts.

"Take," he said, handing Nat a pair of thick felt

trousers, a red wool shirt and a brown sweater.

"Is this a joke?" asked Nat.

He raised an eyebrow.

"No. No joke, Princess. Put on."

"My name is Nat, not Princess."

"Got it, Princess."

She decided to ignore him and concentrate on the felt trousers.

"Wen would have a fit," she said, turning them over in her hands.

"Wen? Fit?"

"You wouldn't understand."

He folded his arms.

"You insult me. I understand. My English is well learned."

Nat sighed and pulled on the hand-knitted socks, fur-lined coat, long pair of leather boots with up-turned toes, and pair of thermal gloves.

She sniffed the coat's sleeve, running her nose all the way down to the gloves.

"This stinks," she said, wrinkling her nose.

"Or you?" said Altan with a smirk. "Here."

He tossed a brown fur hat at her like a frisbee. Her reaction was so quick that she caught it in one hand. A momentary flash of surprise crossed his face. She pulled it down over her ears. She wanted to stick her tongue out at him, but she was too old for that now.

Chapter Forty-One
CONCERN

"I'm most concerned that Nat has still not heard from Jamuka," said Doctor Tang over breakfast.

Wen ran her fingers through her newly pink-coloured hair. She'd got more to worry about than that, but she wasn't about to tell her mum the truth.

"Me too."

Doctor Tang poured a large cup of coffee from the gold pot that sat on their marble kitchen table.

"I sent another message to the Mongolian authorities again late last night, voicing my concern, but they've come back with the same response. We have to verify the location before they will begin an investigation. It is most frustrating."

Wen nodded.

"Tell me again. What kind of search did you say you were doing while you were staying with her?"

"We tried looking for Borjigin contact details in the Hentii Mountains, and when that was hopeless we tried the Ulan Bator region. But there are thousands and thousands of Borjigins, Mum."

"Hmm." She took a sip of coffee, deep in thought. "The longer he is out of contact the more chance there is…"

Wen waited for her mum to complete her sentence. She had already guessed what she was about to say. Wen and Nat had already talked about the possibility of it, but the thought that her practical, scientific mum was about to voice that possibility made her blood run cold.

"More chance of what, Mum?"

Doctor Tang looked up, her brow furrowed.

"That … that perhaps Jamuka has been poisoned too."

Chapter Forty-Two
BIG FREEZE

Nat bent down to pick up her backpack. With so many clothes on she felt like a marshmallow. She reached inside and pulled out Fizz. His eyes snapped open from sleep mode. The moment he saw her they glowed bright green.

"*Location Mongolia,*" he announced.

"That robot?" said Altan, taking a step closer.

Tracking his voice, Fizz looked up at Altan.

Nat's hand curled around her dragon, cradling him protectively. "His name's Fizz."

Altan laughed. "No fizz here, too cold. You have robot-warmer suit?"

"A what?"

"Suit?"

Nat frowned. She didn't like to feel one-upped.

"No," she said quietly.

"We get him one at market."

"Gosh, this is a hullabaloo," said Fred.

Nat looked across to see her trying to squeeze into

a pair of black trousers that only went halfway up her legs. The stitching was straining at the seams.

Altan walked over, grabbed the trousers around the waistband and pulled them up.

"Goodness me, young man, what strength!"

He took no notice, grabbed a knee-high boot and stood at her side. Nat had to laugh as he reached down to grab Fred's foot as if she was a horse. He lifted it, placing it inside the boot and tugged hard. It jammed against Fred's bulging calf and wouldn't budge.

"You need man boots," said Altan, giving up.

Fred ignored him. She picked a long black coat off the floor and pulled it on. It reached halfway down her arms.

"Fizz, photo Fred, send to Wen and Henry," whispered Nat. "Title it 'snow giant'."

Altan stuffed the remaining clothes into a bag and slung it over his shoulder.

"Put robot away. Follow," he said, heading towards the exit.

Nat stuffed Fizz into her coat pocket. As she stepped through the door, she ducked her head against the icy, horizontal wind. How could anyone survive in a place like this? The frigid arctic air felt like needles as she breathed it in. She wanted to flee back into the relative warmth of the airport and find the next flight home.

Up ahead Altan was striding out into the night air. Fred lumbered behind him like a yeti. Nat followed.

They stopped next to an Overrider. Nat had seen shiny new Overriders on the streets of Hong Kong before, but they were nothing like this one. Instead of four wheels it had six, each one bearing a massive metal-studded tyre, which lifted the all-terrain truck high up above the ground. The truck itself was scratched and chipped. The yellow paint had all but worn away leaving a dull sheen of metal glinting under the dim car-park lights. On top sat a roof rack, tightly packed with boxes, making it almost twice its normal height. A big canvas tarpaulin anchored them down. Four giant search lamps framed the windscreen. It was a beast.

Altan opened the door.

"Princess in back," he said to Nat, waving his hand inside.

For a moment she felt like throwing him a one-inch punch but she couldn't be bothered. Better to ignore him. She climbed into the back row of seats where there was just enough room for her to squeeze into a narrow bucket seat that lay between stacks of boxes.

Fred clambered in behind, filling the whole middle row. Altan shoved her crates in at her feet.

"Be careful with those, young man!" sang out Fred in a high operatic voice.

Nat clapped her hands over her ears. It was deafening.

Altan pretended he hadn't heard her. He landed her last crate with a thud on top of the others and slid the door closed. Moments later he jumped into the passenger seat. Next to him, the driver grunted a greeting and started the engine. Nat fumbled in her pocket for Fizz. When she pulled him out, his eyes were heavy-lidded.

"Temperature below zero. Function impaired," he said, his voice slurred and faint.

She wrapped her gloved hand around him, trying to transfer her warmth to him.

"Call Wen and Henry," she said, opening her palm.

His normally sparkly eyes were dull and faded. His wings creaked slowly open.

"*Hai*, what time is it there?" said Wen, blinking into the camera. "Is that a dead fox on your head?"

"Ha ha. Very funny. Sometime in the middle of the night. I don't know exactly," said Nat. "This is the coldest place on the planet."

CRIMSON POISON

"Mum asked if I had a good time with you. I said it was *ding* but we spent all our time searching for Borjigins. She's tried the Mongolian authorities again but they won't start a search until we've got proof of location."

"Hopefully I'll have that soon."

Her screen split. Henry appeared in the other half, his hair sticking out at funny angles.

"Where are you?" He yawned.

Nat smiled. "In an Overrider. Did you finish the postcard? Am I in big trouble?"

"No, Henry did a *ding* job with the beach," said Wen.

"Mummy's going to buy the biggest mansion on the Peak before you get back. It's a monster, and so is she," said Henry.

Nat gulped.

They talked until Fizz's battery ran into the red zone. Nat wiped away the condensation and looked out of the window at snow flurries blowing in swirling patterns.

"Assistance, please," said Fred, swinging her head round, blinding Nat with her head torch.

She thrust a pair of tweezers into Nat's hand.

"Hold this."

Peering over the back of the seat, Nat saw that Fred had set up a mini lab. A rack of test tubes sat on top of a wooden board where a half-dissected plant lay next to a scalpel.

"When I slice through the stem, hold it open."

"What is it?"

"A *Spectaculum lichotis.*"

Nat leaned over the seat, poised with the tweezers. Fred picked up the scalpel and drew it down the stem like a surgeon.

"Hold!" she barked.

Nat reached over and pinched one side of the stem between the tweezers.

"No! There," said Fred, grabbing her hand and repositioning it.

Satisfied, Fred reached into a small bag and brought out an Octozeb. It had been cut in half, only one goggle remaining. She clipped it on to the right lens of her glasses.

"*Ku!* SPIN makes the Octozeb. I'd never have thought of using it for this though," said Nat, happy to see something so familiar.

Fred paused.

"Your company?"

"Yes. It was really my parents' though. They started

it with my Grandpa Walter, my mum's dad."

"I will have to request that you give me a new one for my future expedition – the one that you have committed to most handsomely fund."

Fred bent her head over the stem and started to hum.

"Do you think the Clan has been poisoned?" said Nat, at last daring to ask her burning question.

Fred fell silent for a moment.

"I cannot say as yet what we will discover when we arrive at the camp. But I do fear we must anticipate that some harm has come from the Marbolic poison. It is, ultimately, deadly." She looked back up at Nat. "I will do my very best to find an antidote, but it will take both you and me to do it. Are you with me?"

Chapter Forty-Three
ACTION!

The test had begun. He watched the man race around the compound, and glanced over at the Barzurkan guards, pleased to see their jaws had dropped in amazement. The man was running faster than a cheetah. He was a flash of colour against the white landscape. His feet sent flurries of snow up into the air, his lungs working like a pair of giant bellows.

One of the Barzurkan, armed with a stopwatch, shook his head as he checked the man's times.

"Eight times faster than before," he announced.

"Excellent," said the General, taking another puff on his stogie cigar. He was dressed in a heavy fur coat and hat, bearing the insignia of 14th Battalion. "This is better than I'd hoped. Good work. We can put the rumours to bed now about our weapon and announce our release date. It's time to show the world how the Barzurkan superpower is now super-superpowered."

The General slapped Burilgi hard on the back, and nodded towards one of the guards. The guard stepped forward holding a large briefcase. Another nod and he clicked it open to reveal neat stacks of hundred-dollar bills.

"My deposit," said the General. "How much of this can you make?"

"More than you need, but I must have more Growemup to get a good crop. This weather is killing the plants."

The General inhaled sharply. "That might be difficult."

He shrugged. "I need it. And by the way, my price just went up. I want fifteen million US dollars."

The General paused. He took a step closer to him. "You make the quantity we agreed and in five days I give it to you. But if you fail, you will pay. Understood?"

He nodded, pleased with his clever bargaining. He had the General just where he wanted him.

A soldier stepped forward holding a tray on which were placed several glasses of ice-cold vodka.

Burilgi took one, held up his glass in a toast and swallowed it in a single gulp.

"*Prost.*"

Chapter Forty-Four
THE STEPPE

Nat put on her sunglasses and picked Fizz up off her lap. Only his green snout was peeping out of the all-in-one yellow fake-fur super-heater robot suit that Altan had found for him at the night bazaar on the outskirts of Ulan Bator.

It was a bit of a loose fit, since it was made for the newer robot models. Nat had to tie the heat connectors on to Fizz's wings with string but it was better than nothing.

She climbed stiffly out of the back of the Overrider into the cold air. Even with sunglasses, the light was intense. The flat snowscape stretched out before her as far as the eye could see. There was not a tree, hill, village, person or building in sight. Above, the sky was a clear, piercing blue. A quiver of excitement ran through her. She was finally in Jamuka's homeland.

"A white desert," said Fred. "Just like they said."

Fred was clomping through the snow in her oversized man boots, also picked up by Altan in the night bazaar. They were four sizes too big but at least she could get her feet into them. He had found her a bigger coat too, in red. Out on the snow, Fred looked like a lost Father Christmas.

Nat watched her kneel down and start digging in the snow, like a dog searching for its bone. Altan and the driver were leaning against the Overrider drinking hot tea, looking on with interest.

"Assistant, bring my bag!" she called.

Nat grabbed Fred's leather bag from the back seat and started to tramp across the snow. Her boot slipped on some ice. She landed hard.

"Careful. That bag's got glass in it!" roared Fred.

"Need help, Princess?" said Altan, appearing at her side. He was grinning from ear to ear.

"No, thank you," she said sharply.

He picked up the bag and carried it over to Fred. Nat pushed herself up off the ground and brushed the snow off her coat. Snow! She was going to have to get used to it.

"Fizz, call Wen," she said, brushing down his furry suit.

The tip of his snout glowed orange.

"*Heya*, Nat, I can't see you," said Wen through Fizz's speakers.

"Fizz is in a robot-warmer suit so he can't open his wings."

"That sounds *ding*! How is it going?"

Nat leaned closer in towards Fizz's snout. She didn't want anyone to hear her, especially Altan.

"Freezing but beautiful. Everything's white. I've been told we're going to be out of range soon. No one has bothered to put up any comms links out here so this is probably the last time we can talk."

"Got it. Listen – the wicked witch is up to very bad tricks. You don't have long to find Jamuka and bring him back to stop her."

"Assistant, test tube!" shouted Fred.

Nat looked across the snow. Fred had reached ground level and was scraping off shavings of earth with her penknife.

"And be quick about it!"

"*Ai yah!* Sounds like you've got your hands full," said Wen.

"*Zoinks*, between her and this Altan boy it's not exactly a bag of laughs."

"Hurry up!" warbled Fred.

"You'd better go," said Wen. "Help Fred. Try calling me later, and if it doesn't work, just find Jamuka FAST."

CRIMSON POISON

Wen cut the call. Nat headed across the snow to Fred. She fumbled with the bag's buckles, reached inside and pulled out a wooden box. To unhook the top she had to take off her gloves. The cold bit into her fingers. She grabbed a clean test tube from a rack and handed it to Fred.

"About time," said Fred, grabbing it off her and shoving the earth inside. She held the filled test tube up triumphantly in the air. "Our first specimen!" she sang at the top of her voice.

Altan and the driver burst out laughing. Fred was oblivious.

"Truck ready. We go!" shouted Altan.

Nat silently groaned as she climbed back into the Overrider. She had to fold in her legs to fit behind Fred's seat, which Fred had insisted on pushing back as far as it would go to make herself more comfortable. It was like being squashed in a sardine can.

"Want, Princess?" said Altan, reaching across the seats with a packet of peanut cookies.

"Thanks."

She bit into one and promptly spat it out. It was like eating a piece of old, damp cardboard. She looked at Altan, giving him the evil eye that she had practised so often and so effectively on Henry, but to her surprise he wasn't grinning. His eyes were wide with surprise.

"You no like?"

"No," she said, waiting for him to laugh at her.

He picked one from the top of the packet and crunched down on it.

"They good."

"No they're not, they're inedible."

"Not eat?"

"Exactly. They are utterly not eatable."

Altan frowned, snatching back the packet.

"Oh no you don't," said Fred, grabbing it mid-air. "They'll do very well for me."

Nat's stomach grumbled. If that was the standard of food, she was going to starve.

Chapter Forty-Five
MUTTON STEW

Nat woke up to find that the Overrider had pulled up next to a round white tent. It was a real *ger*, just like the ones she'd seen in photos. Next to it huddled a flock of sheep in a small covered corral. An old motorbike was propped up against the railings. A man and little girl stepped out of the door. They had wide, rosy-cheeked faces and both were dressed in long grey coats. Behind them lay a thick forest.

Altan leapt out of the passenger seat and ran over to them. The man embraced him heartily. They were smiling and laughing.

"Let's hope they've got something on the stove," said Fred, heaving herself out. "I'm starving."

Nat picked Fizz up off her lap.

"Call Wen."

"*Out of range, no communication possible,*" said Fizz, his voice weak.

She sighed. This was it. She was on her own. She pushed down the back of Fred's seat, climbed over and out to the open air.

"Princess," called Altan, waving her over.

She was going to ignore him but the man at his side was smiling broadly at her.

"*Sain baina uu?*" said Nat, with a bow of her head towards the man.

Altan raised an eyebrow in surprise.

"*Sain,*" replied the man, returning the bow.

"You speak Mongolian?" whispered Altan.

"A little," she replied.

"Day one in the life of a native Mongol begins," sang Fred, notebook in hand.

The man's daughter grabbed Nat's hand, pulling her towards the *ger*. They passed in through the door. Inside, the wooden tent frame was painted bright red, with thick felt lining the walls. The stove sat in the middle. Wisps of white smoke drifted upwards and out through the flue. A row of simple beds stood against the walls with an old red dresser beside the largest bed.

Nat's nose wrinkled. The whole tent stank of boiled meat.

The man's wife was sitting stirring a bubbling stew in an ancient cauldron over the central stove. She nodded a greeting.

CRIMSON POISON

"Sit," said Altan, signalling for them to take a seat on the cushions that lined the floor.

Altan and the man spoke in low voices while Fred was bent over her notebook. The mother passed Nat a steaming bowl. She bowed her head in thanks and looked at the pale milky liquid swirling around inside. A stink of bad cheese wafted up.

She took a sip. Its smoky, salty taste made her gag. Fred, however, gulped hers down in one go.

"Delicious!" she sang, handing the bowl back to the mother. "More, please!"

The mother looked up in alarm. Then she stood up and began to ladle steaming hot, brown, oily stew into bowls. Grey balls of something were floating, half submerged, on top. Altan and the man started to slurp it down. Fred and the little girl tucked in too.

Nat tentatively pushed one of the balls to the edge of the bowl. Using her finger she rolled it up into her mouth. She bit into it. A hot spurt of fat filled her mouth. The dough ball contained old mutton. It tasted like elastic bands. If the salty tea was bad then this was a thousand times worse. She quietly spat the half-chewed fatty lump out into her hand and popped it in her pocket. The little girl giggled.

"Princess not like?" said Altan.

Nat blushed. She'd been caught out, and of all people it had to be by Altan. Everyone was staring at her now. There was only thing for it. She put on her best smile, dipped her finger into the stew and fished out another mutton ball. Keeping her smile fixed she opened her mouth and dropped the ball into her mouth.

She bit down into it, trying to convince herself that she was really eating a potsticker at the Lucky Cat restaurant.

"Mmm," she managed to murmur.

A big Mongolian man came barrelling in through the door. While everyone turned to him Nat swiftly took the fat ball out of her mouth and stuffed it into her pocket with the other one.

"We go," said Altan, already on his feet. "Horses."

"Horses?" said Nat in alarm.

Altan clicked his tongue as if urging an imaginary horse into a trot.

"Horses," he said.

"They have minds of their own, if you ask me," grumbled Fred.

Nat swallowed hard. No one had mentioned anything about having to ride a horse.

"Go," said Altan, heading out of the door.

CRIMSON POISON

Nat handed her bowl back to the mother. She followed Altan to find three men wearing tall fur hats and ankle-length coats now standing at the treeline. They greeted Altan warmly and launched into a loud conversation, waving their arms about, pointing at Fred and Nat.

"Come, singer and Princess!" shouted Altan, waving her and Fred over.

"This boy takes a few liberties, doesn't he? I think we should find a suitable name for him too," said Fred.

Nat smiled. *Monkey-brain* was the first name that sprang to mind, but she bit back the words. There would be plenty of time to think of a better one. She slung her backpack over her shoulder and started to trudge through the deep snow.

The driver revved the Overrider's engine and drove off, leaving a deep stillness in his wake. Nat stepped into the gloom of the forest. Three dark, stocky horses with thick coats stood waiting, swishing their tails backwards and forwards, their breath forming mini clouds of crystals in the air. They were tacked up, ready to ride.

"You don't seriously expect us to use wooden saddles, do you?" said Fred.

Altan frowned in confusion. Fred approached the

closest horse, tapped its saddle and pointed to the trees.

"Wood," he said with a shrug.

Fred snorted. A nearby horse danced back in alarm. Altan held up his hand. "Quiet. Horses scared. Princess, come."

Nat grunted and headed over to where he was holding a small brown horse. Fear gripped her, but she didn't want Altan to see. This was a real, live animal, just like Dragon Khan. It wasn't a robot or a Slider.

The horse swung its head round, sizing her up. Nat gulped.

"Up," said Altan, holding the stirrup for her.

She lifted her boot and slotted it into the stirrup. The horse moved forward, forcing her to hop alongside. She felt a hand push her up, launching her over into the saddle. The horse moved again. She grabbed on to the reins, terrified she might fall.

Altan steadied the horse. "Princess no ride?"

His eyes were wide with amazement. Nat shook her head. She wasn't going to tell him about her asthma, her allergies and lack of any real contact ever with live animals except for Jamuka's songbird, Gobi.

Altan walked the horse forward a couple of paces. Nat lurched backwards in the saddle.

"Like this," he said, showing her how to use the reins.

Nat dearly wished she had brought her Slider with her. In high hover mode, it could easily have travelled over the snow.

"*Temperature below zero. Function impaired,*" bleated Fizz, who she'd just clipped on to the side of her coat.

She glanced down to see that his eyes had changed from green to pale blue. Even with the super robot-warmer suit he was fading fast. Holding the reins in one hand, she used the other to stuff him back inside her fur coat, close to her chest.

"I will crush it!" said Fred.

Nat turned to see Fred sizing up the biggest of the horses. Its ears were pinned back as it rolled its eyes at her. A second later a man appeared leading a huge carthorse through the trees.

"Big horse for big singer," said Altan.

The horse train moved off. Altan led the way with Nat following. Her horse was walking at a snail's pace, which suited her perfectly.

"Kick it on!" urged Fred, riding up behind her.

"No," said Nat.

Fred trotted alongside her, leaned down and gave

Nat's horse a slap on the rear. It shot forward like a rocket.

"Help!" cried Nat.

She clutched on to the pommel of the saddle. Luckily she could not fall off because Altan had tied her boots to the stirrups.

Chapter Forty-Six
ALMOST ENCOUNTER

"Now, here we are in the magnificent turn-of-the-century sitting room. It commands a glorious central position in the house and, of course, boasts breathtaking views over the harbour," said Mr Wing, directing them over to the floor-to-ceiling windows.

Henry traipsed after Prissy and Aunt Vera as they squealed in delight. Their sharp heels dug into the priceless rug as they rushed over to take in the view. They had been looking at houses since eight o'clock in the morning; it was now late afternoon. Henry was bored and exhausted.

Mr Wing, estate agent to the rich and famous, wore a grey silk suit and a white shirt with a purple tie, and everything about him reminded Henry of sharks circling, hunting their prey, in those nature films on Channel Fifty-Six.

"This is, like, so it!" shrieked Prissy, her glitter cat robot clipped on to her shoulder, filming everything.

"Just wait till I show Candy. She's going to be so jealous!"

Aunt Vera clapped her hands. "We'll take it, Mr Wing. It feels like home already."

Mr Wing smiled, flashing his pearly-white, perfect teeth, and looked down at his gold watch. "I think a celebration is in order. I suggest we move to The Peninsula where we can discuss details over some champagne – my treat, of course, ladies."

Henry sighed. The day had just got a lot longer.

The hotel manager greeted Mr Wing like an old friend and escorted them to a central table in the bar. Aunt Vera's eyes lit up when she saw a bottle of vintage Dom Perignon in a silver ice bucket awaiting them.

"Mr Wing, you rotten spoiler," she said, giggling girlishly.

Henry slumped down in a blue velvet armchair. One sip of champagne and he knew his mother would want to stay for hours. The waiter carefully popped the cork and poured their glasses.

"Henry darling, a Shirley Temple for being such a good boy?"

Henry's cheeks burned at the humiliation of being offered such a girly drink and he took a quick look around the bar in case any of his friends might be there.

"A Popko juice, please," he said.

"Sir, I see you have your robot with you. Might you enjoy this?" said the waiter, leaning across to press the under arm of Henry's chair.

The velvet cover slid back to reveal a flat, disc-shaped screen. Henry placed NutNut on top. The robot's eyes lit up bright blue. His tail flattened against his back and his screen appeared.

"Wow, it's the latest Scowler Stone!" said Henry, reading the movie listings.

"All the latest releases. Welcome to The Peninsula," said the waiter.

Maybe being at The Peninsula wasn't so bad after all. Henry lounged back in his chair.

"Henry. Take my photo," snapped Prissy, thrusting her glitter cat at him.

"I'm busy."

Prissy pouted. He sighed and pointed the cat's eyes at her.

"Not so close," she said.

He leaned back. Prissy held up her glass, tossed back her hair and smiled, all for the camera. He took a load of shots and handed the glitter cat back. She immediately checked them out.

"Hmm, take a couple more. Make sure you get some background so my friends know where I am."

Henry lifted the cat again. Suddenly, to his horror, through the holographic viewfinder he spotted Doctor Tang sitting a few seats away. She was with two friends, sipping tea from a china cup. Henry reached under the glitter cat's neck and switched it to manual. He scrolled through the pictures and used the blur function to mask out Doctor Tang's face. Thank goodness Prissy hadn't noticed.

"Here," he said.

Prissy had a look.

"*Ku*. It's obvious where I am," she said. "Candy and Caprice are going to be, like, *green* with envy."

Aunt Vera and Mr Wing had their heads bent over a piece of paper on which they were negotiating the price of the house. There were so many zeros, it made Henry's mind boggle.

"I'm going to the ladies' room," said Prissy, getting to her feet. "I bet there'll be loads of freebies."

Henry panicked. She would spot Doctor Tang. He jumped up.

"Me too."

"Come on then," said Prissy irritably.

Prissy turned right but Henry leapt into her path and barged into her, pushing her in the other direction.

"Henry, stop it!" she said, brushing him off.

"But I want to go by the kaleidoscope."

"Well, I don't."

"Oh, for goodness' sake, take him by the kaleidoscope, Prissy. And stop causing a scene," said Aunt Vera, glancing up over the top of her reading glasses.

Prissy huffed and stomped off with Henry beside her. Henry knew she was furious with him for cramping her style as she sashayed through the room, but he stuck to her like glue.

"So?" she said, when they reached a rainbow-coloured wall. "Does baby Henry want a go?"

"A quick one," he said, opening the door set into the wall. "But you have to come too."

"No way. I'll see you back at the table," she said, stalking off towards the ladies' toilet.

"I'll tell Mum about you and Candy going to Bongo's…"

"How do you know I've been there?" She spun round.

"Nat and I watched you through the window. We saw you and Candy with your needles."

"Mum will never believe you."

Henry held out his squirrel. "NutNut, play Bongo Prissy visit."

Up came a shot of Prissy and Candy entering the doors of a rainbow-coloured shop. Once inside, the girls were greeted by a dark-haired man dressed in a long, stripy knitted coat and hat. He hugged them before leading them over to a table laden with balls of wool in every colour of the rainbow. The girls sat down and the man passed them each a piece of knitting from a basket. They started to click the needles together, chatting and giggling.

"You know what Mummy thinks of knitters," said Henry. "She hates them more than she does hippies."

"You wouldn't dare!" said Prissy.

Out of the corner of his eye he saw Doctor Tang throw back her head and laugh.

He narrowed his eyes. "Try me!"

Prissy pushed past him through the door. "This had better be quick."

They entered a small, round room. The floor, walls and ceiling were mirrored. A circular window looked out over the city.

"Go on then," huffed Prissy.

Henry stepped forward and pressed the big green

button below the window. Another piece of glass slid out of the wall over the window. In between two sheets of thick glass lay pockets of multicoloured glass beads. As it began to rotate, the beads started to shift, creating psychedelic patterns.

"This is definitely the best one," said Henry.

Prissy stood with her arms folded across her chest, staring at the patterns.

"One go and we're done, right?"

Henry nodded, hoping that Doctor Tang would be gone.

Five minutes later they were on their way back but Doctor Tang was still with her friends. Henry waited for Prissy to go into the ladies' before whipping out NutNut to call Wen.

"*Ai yah!*" said Wen, hearing his news.

The toilet door opened and Prissy reappeared, her lips coated in a thick layer of pink lipgloss. Henry cut the call, hiding NutNut behind his back.

"You didn't have to wait," said Prissy, glaring at him.

"I didn't want to get lost."

"You are so lame," she hissed, grabbing him by the arm.

Back at the table, Henry was relieved to find his

mother and Mr Wing still in conversation. Noting that Doctor Tang was still in her seat he slumped in his armchair in front of an enormous glass of Popko juice. Prissy started studying the floorplan of their new home on her mother's FastPad so he ducked under the table with NutNut.

"I'm back at my seat, Wen," he whispered.

"I've come up with a plan. Watch," she said.

Henry sat back up and looked over his mother's bent head. Doctor Tang was still sipping tea. Suddenly she stopped, reached into her bag and pulled out her phone. Henry watched her smile change to a deep frown. She stood up from the table, picked up her bag and jacket, and headed towards the exit, across the room.

Henry gulped.

His mother and Mr Wing were still busy, heads locked, and Prissy had her nose stuck in the FastPad. He held his breath. Doctor Tang was now walking directly towards their table before coming to a stop right next to them. She checked her phone again. Henry thought he might faint; he ducked back under the table. He saw her shiny pumps start heading across the carpet towards the lobby and let his breath out so loudly that Aunt Vera looked up.

CRIMSON POISON

"Are you all right, Henry?" she asked, seeing his bright-red face.

Henry nodded.

"My gosh. Wasn't that Doctor Tang?" said Mr Wing in a gossipy tone.

Aunt Vera smiled smugly. "Oh no. Doctor Tang's at her beach house in Tai Long Wan," she said. "I should know because my niece is staying with them."

Chapter Forty-Seven
SADDLE SORE

Altan undid the ropes. Nat swung a wobbly leg over the saddle and landed with a thud in the snow. Her horse put its head down and nosed her, its hot breath defrosting her face. She lay there, staring up at its nostrils, wondering if she would ever be able to walk again. They'd been riding for hours. The saddle was the hardest thing she had ever sat on. It had rubbed her legs raw and her bottom was numb.

Altan offered her a hand up.

"Leave me alone," she growled, feeling that he was somehow to blame.

He shrugged and led his horse off towards the corral. Fred came striding across the snow carrying her two crates. She stopped where Nat lay, put the crates down, grasped Nat's hand and hauled her up to her feet.

"No time to rest. I need you to help carry these," she said.

Two hours later Nat lay exhausted on a rollout

mattress next to a stove in one of the *gers*. She wasn't alone. Fred, Altan and a family of five – a mother, father, two young girls and a boy – were all fanned out across the tent floor, buried under thick wool blankets.

She hadn't been this tired in a very long time, not since she, Jamuka and Ah Wong had sailed up the coast of China last summer. Then she'd been exhausted from her role as deckhand, hauling ropes and sails, since the *Junko*'s rigging computer had broken two days into the trip.

Closing her eyes she became acutely aware of the crackle of the wood burning in the stove and the low hum of breathing. It was a far cry from the bedtime sounds she had grown up with – the whistling wind, Gobi's sweet birdsong and the ocean lapping at the hull of the *Junko*. She missed the swaying motion that had lulled her to sleep every night. She missed her home; she missed Jamuka.

Reaching under her blanket she pulled out Fizz, who remained swaddled in his robot-warmer suit. She tapped him once on his snout, activating his silent mode. His eyes snapped open. They had a warm emerald glow to them, something she'd not seen since they had stepped out into the arctic air at the airport in Ulan Bator.

Pulling the blanket up over her head so that she didn't disturb Fred, who lay snoring away next to her, she unzipped and removed his suit. Her heart leapt as she watched his wings slowly unfurl. In the darkness of the under-blanket world his wings shimmered, each scale throwing off a tiny pinprick of diamond-like light. She'd forgotten just how beautiful he was. His screen flickered, lighting up, not to its normal luminescent brightness, but to a dim, powered-down version.

"Play Gobi song movie. Keep silent mode," she whispered into his ear.

Instantly she was transported on board the *Junko*. Its deck appeared on screen. Hong Kong's skyline towered up in the background. Wen and Jamuka were seated on cushions with Gobi's cage on the decking between them. Wen's hair was bright yellow with tangerine stripes, the same colour as her dress. Jamuka was dressed in a black suit, wearing his signature round, mirrored sunglasses. Both were studying SmartSheets, which they held in their hands.

Nat didn't need sound; she'd watched it at least a hundred times before. They were rehearsing their words for "Gobi, Gobi, my name's not Moby", which she and Wen had written for their school performance last year. Neither of them could compose music so they'd opted to do a rap version instead.

A smile twitched at her lips as she watched Jamuka and Wen start rapping to Gobi. Gobi started to flap his wings and join in. The song played along in Nat's head, as did the gales of laughter at the end. All she wanted was to be back there now…

It felt like she'd just dozed off when she was woken by a deafening clatter of metal pots. She opened her eyes to find that everyone else was already up and gone. Mattresses had been rolled away, leaving a lone woman with a couple of cooking pots on the stove. A mutton fug hung in the air.

Nat pushed herself up. She unfolded her coat, which she'd used as her pillow, and slipped it on. Her legs were as stiff as boards. She clambered to her feet like an old woman, wincing at the thought of sitting in the saddle again. Every bone and muscle in her body ached.

The woman looked up from her stirring as Nat hobbled over to the door and pulled on her boots. Nat managed a faint smile and bowed her head before stepping out through the door. A refreshing smell of woodsmoke and horses greeted her.

She pulled her hat down low over her face and ears to try and block out the icy cold. She flapped her arms about like a bird, as she endeavoured to warm up. It was another crystal-clear day. The sun was creeping up above a forest of pine trees. Out here somewhere was Jamuka and his Clan, and the Tumen Vachir. A feeling of dread washed over her. What if she was too late? What if … what if … she dare not think it, but it popped up anyway … what if they were already dead?

Voices were coming from the direction of the forest. She blinked away a mist of involuntary tears and crunched her way over the snow towards the treeline. A few steps in she came to a makeshift gate in a wall of pine branches. She opened it to find a small corral where Altan and another man were saddling up the horses.

"*Öglöönii mend,*" said Altan.

Nat nodded, unsure of what he meant.

"Watch, learn, Princess," he said.

He showed Nat how to position the saddle and let her tighten the girth. Next came the bridle. As Nat put it over the horse's ears she let out a deep sigh.

"How long do we ride?" she said.

"Day," said Altan.

"A whole day to get to the Clan?"

"Yes, Princess."

She let out a groan. It was thickly layered with a growing despair.

"Too long," she said.

Altan shrugged and looked up at the sky.

"Long ride to Clan, Princess."

"Stop calling me Princess, you, you…" In her frustration she found herself lost for words. "You utterly annoying altapottamus!"

"Altap…?" said Altan, raising his eyebrows.

A roar of laughter erupted behind them, making them both jump.

"By Jove, that is genius, young lady!" said Fred, lumbering across the snow. "We have discovered a new species – the altapottamus!"

Altan narrowed his eyes. "You fun make?"

Fred slapped him hard on the back. "No, we species make! Now then, I am fuelled on salty tea, so let's get going, shall we?"

Chapter Forty-Eight
MA HUANG

They were moving steadily through the trees when the snow flurries started. Altan was in the lead. He hadn't spoke to them since the altapottamus incident. Nat wondered how he knew where they were going. Everywhere looked the same. The sky had clouded over with a grey blanket, the wind had picked up and icy flakes now began to fall, pricking her face like tiny needles.

Despite the horse's body heat, Nat was chilled to the bone. The air seemed to thin the higher they went and she began to feel a familiar tightening in her chest. She slowed her horse and took Fizz out of her pocket.

"Fizz, air," she commanded, putting his snout to her mouth.

A tiny whiff of medication seeped out into her mouth.

"*Too cold. Malfunction,*" said Fizz, his voice now dull and flat.

Fear gripped her like a vice.

CRIMSON POISON

"Help!" she wheezed, reining her horse to a stop.

Fred trotted up behind. "No time for potty stops—"
She stopped and took one look at Nat's deathly pale
face as Nat whispered, "Can't breathe," before falling
off her horse.

"Altan!" shouted Fred, jumping down to the
ground. "Joint fir, quick."

Altan continued on his horse. He didn't turn round.
"Joint?" he shouted.

Fred pulled out her notebook from inside her hat.
She took off her gloves and quickly thumbed through
it.

"*Ma huang*," she yelled, striding off into the forest.

This time Altan turned his head. The moment he
saw Nat on the ground he reined his horse about and
came galloping back. He drew up sharply, his horse's
hooves spraying up snow in Nat's face.

"*Ma huang*," he said, jumping down.

He put his hand under her armpit, hauling her up
into a sitting position. Her nose whistled and her
airways wheezed as she tried to suck in tiny wisps of
air. He grabbed dry wood from his saddlebags and
quickly made a fire. He took a small pot, filled it with
fresh snow and placed it over the flames. Nat heard
the crackle of burning wood. A fire wouldn't help.

She didn't want to die here, like this…

Altan spread out a goatskin next to the fire and pulled Nat on to it. Kneeling next to her, he took off his fur-lined coat and put it around her shoulders.

"Look," he said, taking her hands in his.

Nat forced herself to look up. Dark spots swam in front of her eyes. Altan inhaled deeply through his nose like a snuffling pig, and then out through his mouth. He repeated it.

"You same," he said.

Nat shook her head. She was dizzy now. Her airways were quickly closing up.

"Yes, Princess," he said, fixing his eyes on hers.

She wheezed in once and out once.

"More!" he shouted.

Nat tried again.

"More!" he roared.

His brown eyes locked on to hers; he didn't blink. His face bore deep furrows of concentration. She felt like she was being hypnotised.

"*Ma huang*," said Fred, triumphantly marching up to the fire waving a long, spindly branch. "Otherwise known as joint fir, the oldest remedy in the world for asthma. Now we need to make it swiftly into tea."

She thrust it into the pot of boiling water until the

liquid turned a murky-brown colour.

"Drink this," said Fred, holding a bowl to Nat's lips. "Small sips, please, but you must drink it as hot as possible."

Trying to drink at the same time as breathe was pure torture. The tea burned her lips, her tongue, but Fred held it steady, barking at her to keep drinking.

The minutes ticked by. Nat drank three bowlfuls. She was drowning in tea but the wheezing was slowing. She managed a weak smile.

"Thank you," said Nat, looking from Fred to Altan. "I'm sorry I called you an altapottamus earlier."

His eyes darted from hers to the ground between them. Instead of a princess quip he silently bowed his head.

"Now then, young man, all this activity has made me ravenous. Let's have some of that mutton fat tea before we head off," said Fred.

Altan stood up and walked over to his horse. Nat looked out across the forest floor. That had been a close call. Without Fred and Altan she'd probably be dead by now. She reached inside her pocket. It was empty. Fizz?

Her mind flashed back to him in her hand as he had tried to blast her the medication. She must have dropped him to the ground. She pushed herself up to her feet and took a few shaky steps to where her horse was tethered.

A long, mournful howl came echoing through the trees, making the hairs on the back of her neck stand up. The horses whinnied, shifting uneasily in the snow.

"What the blazes is—" said Fred.

Altan threw his head back and let out a long, deep howl.

"Extraordinary," said Fred, reaching for her notebook. "It must be a communication tool."

Nat spotted Fizz lying up ahead in the snow, his green snout peeking up out of the yellow robot-warmer suit. Fear rooted her to the spot. Wolves. Real, live wolves, just like the ones Jamuka had described in his bedtime stories. This time not one, but two distinctively different howls came sounding through the trees. Adrenalin started to pulse through her veins, making her hyper alert.

Altan howled back again.

"They come," he said, kicking snow on to the fire, extinguishing the flames.

"Wolves?" said Nat, her heart beating fast.

"We ride," he said.

CRIMSON POISON

She stumbled across the snow and picked up Fizz. Despite the suit his eyes were now locked closed, in power-down mode.

Altan grabbed her hand and hurried her to his horse.

"I can't ride yours," she said as he hoisted her up into the saddle. Looking down, the ground seemed a long way away.

"I can," he said, jumping up behind her.

Before Nat could protest he kicked his horse on. She shot back against his chest.

"Hold on," he said, reaching around her and taking the reins.

She hooked her hands on to the pommel, gripping tight, as Altan rode over to her own horse and grabbed its tether.

"*Chooooo!*" he urged.

Both horses broke into a gallop. She closed her eyes against the wind and snow while Altan expertly rode through the trees at a lightning pace.

The pine trees started to thicken. He slowed them to a trot, before finally coming to a halt in a small clearing.

"Whoa!" bellowed Fred, thundering up beside them.

Her feet shot out of the stirrups, she threw one leg

over the saddle and came crashing down to land in the snow. She lifted the top crate off the back of the saddle and started rummaging inside.

"My samples are being compromised with all this frantic movement," she grumbled, holding up a test tube with a brown froth inside. "My *Dahlicus mosanti* shouldn't look like this."

"Shhh," said Altan, his finger to his lips.

Fred shot him a look of thunder and turned back to her crate.

Altan signalled for Nat to dismount. The moment she landed he waved her away from the horse. She took a few steps back, unsure where she should go. Too far away and she might get eaten by a wolf. She turned to ask him but he was now holding his horse's head in his hands, looking straight into its eyes, just as he had done with her during the asthma attack. The horse pulled back for a moment, uncomfortable at the intrusion, but a sudden quiver ran through its body. Its gaze fell comfortably on Altan's face.

"What are you doing?" she whispered.

"Ready for wolf," he said, moving on to Fred's horse. "When wolf come, stay."

Just as he said this, an enormous shadow came bounding through the trees. A jet-black wolf hurled itself at Altan, knocking him flat. Nat screamed as the two of them fell to the ground, wrestling in a knot of arms and legs. Fred's horse reared up and galloped off into the forest.

Suddenly the wolf stopped, his golden eyes coming to rest on Nat's face. She turned to flee.

"Stay," said Altan.

Looking back she saw the wolf looking at her. It was as if he could see right into her very being. All breath left her. Her heart was banging like a drum against her chest. He was tall, nearly shoulder height.

He lifted a large paw and started to lope towards her. Altan made a deep guttural sound from the base of his throat. The wolf stopped in its tracks. Now it was only metres away from her, its gaze unflinching. She was rooted to the spot, more terrified than she had ever been before in her life. Altan made the sound again; this time the wolf turned and loped back to where he was standing.

"In…cre…di…ble," sang Fred, making notes in her book from a good distance away.

"His name Jebe," said Altan.

The wolf lay down at his side, tipped its head back and howled.

"Jebe say you Clan, Princess," said Altan, folding

his arms across his chest.

"That is because she is," said a familiar voice as a horse came galloping through the trees.

Chapter Forty-Nine
JEBE

"Jamuka!" cried Nat, running to him. "You're alive!"

Jamuka dismounted. She flew into his arms, burying her face in his coat. She had never been as pleased to see anyone in her whole life. He held her tight.

"Yes, I'm alive, Bao Bao," he said, not letting her go. "However did you get here?"

"I've been to Borneo and I've found Fred who's a friend of Doctor Tang and she's a doctor so she can help. She knows all about Marbolic and Tumen Vachir—"

"My samples are all in jeopardy," interrupted Fred, who marched up to Jamuka and thrust a test tube under his nose. A deep-red liquid fizzed. "See this? Quite ruined."

Jebe sprang to his feet and made his way across to Fred. Jamuka made the same guttural sound as Altan. Nat watched in amazement as the wolf, now just a metre away from Fred, sat down, dropping his head on his paws.

For once Fred was silent. She held the test tube above her head like a statue.

Jamuka bowed his head. "I apologise. It is an honour that you have come all this way to help us."

He made another sound, a high-pitched grunt, and Jebe came to sit at his side. Nat was now right beside the wolf but it ignored her, licking his paws.

Somewhat mollified, Fred extended her hand. "Yes, well. Fred Fairlight," she said. "Pleased to make your acquaintance."

Jebe growled. Fred quickly withdrew her hand.

"Uncle," said Altan, making a sweeping bow.

They exchanged words swiftly in Mongolian, glancing up at the sky as they spoke.

"The storm is closing in; we must leave," said Jamuka. "Stay close together. Fred, ride at the back with Altan. Bao Bao, come with me. Jebe will lead the way."

"Will you help me get my horse?" Nat whispered to Jamuka. It stood over on the other side of the clearing.

"Go alone. Jebe needs to get used to you."

She took a deep breath. The moment she stepped away from Jamuka, the wolf got to his feet and started to follow her.

"Keep walking," said Jamuka. "With purpose.

Show no fear."

Every step felt as if it might be her last. Jebe drew level alongside. She faltered.

"Keep going," he said.

Suddenly Jebe nosed her gloved hand.

"Aaagh!" she squealed, jumping back in fright.

The wolf growled, opening its jaws.

A deep roar came from both Altan and Jamuka. Jebe whined and lay down on the ground.

"Jebe is trying to bond, Bao Bao," said Jamuka, coming to her rescue. "Take three deep breaths and give him your hand."

Nat shook her head. "He'll bite it off."

"If he was going to bite it off, he'd have done so by now."

She gulped. "This is not what you said in my bedtime stories…"

Jamuka walked over to her. "That is because I grew up with the pack. Please, trust me."

She inhaled and exhaled deeply but it wasn't helping. All she could do was stare at Jebe, wondering if Jamuka's plan was going to work.

"Hand?" said Jamuka.

She lifted it and placed it in his. He pulled off her glove.

"What are you doing?" she said, snatching it away.

He removed both his gloves.

"The scent on your skin will imprint much more strongly without your gloves on."

Nat looked up at Jamuka. He took her hands in his.

"Trust me," he said.

He directed her to kneel with him on the snow in front of Jebe.

"Put out your hand," he whispered.

She closed her eyes, unable to look at the big black head so close to her own. Trembling, she held out her right hand. Warm breath was followed by a wet nose pushing up under her palm.

"Good. Move your hand slowly to his chest," he whispered.

She opened one eye. Slowly she moved her hand under the wolf's chin. The fur felt thick and warm. Jebe's golden eyes closed for a moment, his head coming to rest on her hand.

"Now draw back slowly," he said.

She withdrew her hand. Jebe's eyes opened. He looked at her and his tail started to thump the snow.

Chapter Fifty
DESCENT

Burilgi cut the engine and climbed off the snowmobile. It probably wasn't the wisest decision to head down the valley during a blizzard but it was his only chance to come before the harvest, when he'd be working around the clock.

Even in the dark he knew exactly where he was. A childhood of hunting and playing in these woods had left an indelible map in his mind. He unhooked the small backpack, pulled out his bottle of *airag* and took a large swig. The fire spread in his belly. He was ready for anything.

Chapter Fifty-One
THE CAMP

"Do your aunt and uncle know you're here, Bao Bao?" said Jamuka.

"Kind of," said Nat, squirming in the saddle.

They were riding side by side through the forest, headed to camp.

"Start from the beginning, from when I left. We have plenty of time."

Nat took a deep breath.

"OK, so, they took me shopping to Shan-xi…" she began.

The light was beginning to fade when she finished her tale. She turned to Jamuka, waiting for a response, but it was met with silence. She felt crushed.

"You have shown great courage, Bao Bao," he said finally. "You took a dangerous path to get here and I feel a great weight of responsibility on my part for what you have gone through. I never thought that Aunt Vera could be so grasping. But I am deeply disappointed that they think you are somewhere that you are not. Deception is a low game."

Nat's shoulders slumped.

"Sorry. But if I had told the truth, I would never have been allowed to come, and you could have been dead, and I need you to come back to Hong Kong quickly…"

He moved his horse in close alongside and held out his gloved hand. She reached tentatively across. He took her hand in his.

"Let us look to the future. Our search will continue to find the source of the Clan's sickness, and when we have found and stopped it we will return to Hong Kong to deal with your aunt."

"But what if we're too late and she's got guardianship of me?"

He squeezed her hand. "We will fight back and win."

They came out of the treeline to the top of a mountain pass. Snow flurries whipped up and danced in the open air. Jamuka let go.

"We're about to descend into the valley of the Khan. You'll need to hold tight on to your saddle."

Her horse pitched forward down a steep path. Any thoughts of Aunt Vera vanished, as she had to concentrate hard, gripping tight with her knees, so as not to fall out of the saddle.

Just when she thought she couldn't hang on any longer, they entered the camp. A circle of *gers* loomed like giant marshmallows under a fresh dusting of snow. The place was deserted except for a herd of goats bleating softly under the trees.

Nat's legs wobbled as they hit the ground. Her fingers were stiff. It had been a long, hard ride. She lifted the reins over her horse's head and patted him, her head coming to rest on his neck. He snorted, nuzzling her coat, his warm breath clouding up into the air.

"Untack and feed your horse, Bao Bao," said Jamuka.

Her fingers fumbled with the leather straps. The buckles felt like lead weights. She was so tired she could barely get a grip. Steam rose off her horse's back as she dragged off the saddle and felt blanket. They felt heavier than one of the *Junko*'s sails.

"Here," said Jamuka, taking them off her. "Lead him into the corral."

Nat took the rope. She was just entering the corral when Fred hit the top note of the octave that she was trilling up through. The goats bleated in fright, bolting at Nat and her horse. The horse reared, tearing the rope from Nat's hand. It jumped the fence. Nat screamed. A sudden loud roar echoed through the trees. Jebe bounded past her, driving the goats and horse back inside.

The moment his job was done he came to Nat and sat down next to her. He looked up at her, his head cocked to one side. She was trembling from head to toe.

"Good, Bao Bao. He is now your protector," said Jamuka.

The wolf insistently nosed her gloved hand. Nat had no idea what he wanted. Robots were so much more straightforward, and so much less scary.

He turned, loped over to a mound of snow and started to paw it. Nat blinked. Something stirred underneath. She dared herself to follow but stopped in her tracks when she spotted a pair of golden eyes peeking out.

"Qara," said Jamuka, joining her. "Qara, the female alpha wolf."

Another wolf head popped up out of a mound of snow a little further away.

"Tegus," he said.

"Aren't they frozen under there?"

"Quite the opposite. The snow provides insulation

for them – like an Eskimo in an igloo. Come, there's someone who wants to meet you."

He led her over to the nearest *ger* and opened the door. Inside an ancient, wizened woman was hunched over a pot on the stove.

"This is Gan," he said, removing his hat.

"Gran?"

"Gan. I grew up with her. We are the same age."

"But she looks a million years older than you," whispered Nat.

"Life here is harsh."

"*Sain baina uu?*" said Nat, remembering her manners.

The woman looked up.

"*Sain*," she whispered, before focusing back on the pot.

"Some of the salty tea would be good. Then we can get straight to work," said Fred, stomping in.

She removed her hat. A flurry of snow fell as she shook out her mop of unruly grey curls. The gloves came off next, then the coat. They landed in an untidy pile.

"Crates, please, assistant," she said, sitting down.

Nat sighed. "I don't think I can move."

"I get. You promise no singing," said Altan from

the doorway.

Fred sniffed. "My talent is wasted upon your ears."

There was a rasping cough from behind a curtain, which hung from the *ger*'s wooden frame.

"Aunt Tolui," said Jamuka.

He beckoned for Nat to follow. Behind the curtain in a narrow bed lay a tiny, shrunken, white-haired lady buried under a mountain of blankets. Nat realised with shock it was the aunt who had brought Jamuka up after his parents died, the fast rider and brave hunter. Even more alarming was that she was the very same old woman from her nightmare about the red petals.

"Aunt Tolui?" whispered Jamuka.

Her eyes flickered open. She spoke quietly in Mongolian, no more than a whisper.

"Come closer," he said, standing back to allow Nat to lean in.

Aunt Tolui's watery eyes crinkled into a smile when she saw her. Nat reached down and took a gentle hold of her frail hand. It was ice cold and papery.

Aunt Tolui spoke low and hoarse.

"She says you have answered her call and that it is good to see you. You are like a granddaughter to her," translated Jamuka.

Nat smiled, her heart swelling at the word "granddaughter". Aunt Tolui's eyes flickered closed. She was nearly asleep when a coughing fit racked her body. Gan shuffled over and handed Jamuka a bowl of salty tea. Nat moved out of the way. He gently lifted her head, bringing the bowl to her lips. She took a tiny sip and lay back on the pillow.

"She is the one who sent the package containing the petal," said Jamuka quietly. "The sickness has got hold of her and, I fear, her time is near."

Chapter Fifty-Two
QUESTION TIME

Nat, Altan, Jamuka and Fred sat huddled around the stove eating a supper of watery goat stew. Nat chewed on the meat. It was a definite improvement on mutton.

The door opened. An icy blast cut through the tent as three men strode in.

"My father, Tabin," said Altan, introducing them to a man with a wispy black beard.

"Temur," said Jamuka, introducing a man who looked like a younger version of himself.

The last man seemed to fill the tent. He was a big, square man with a bull-like face.

"Buqa," said Jamuka.

He issued a grunt.

Fred burped loudly in response.

Everyone turned.

"Splendid meal. Now, is everyone ready for their interviews? Does anyone speak English?" she asked Jamuka.

"I will translate," he said.

She tore several pages out of her notebook and passed them to Nat, along with a pencil she had tucked behind her ear.

"Please take notes. We mustn't miss a thing."

Nat used her wool shirt to clean some grease off the pencil.

"Right, first off, how many people have died? How many are sick? Men, women, children, wolves – I need names and ages. Then I need symptoms."

Nat pulled Fizz out of her pocket to record. His eyes flickered open. There was a gasp around the tent. She looked up to see the Clan wide-eyed at her dragon's appearance.

"He is one of the first robots they have ever seen," said Jamuka.

Nat unzipped his robot-warmer suit and took him out. Another gasp as he unfurled his wings. She felt like a magician.

"Let them have a closer look," said Jamuka.

Nat was about to pass him round when Fred boomed out, "This is not a circus! Get on with the task at hand, assistant!"

Jamuka nodded at Nat. She sat back down.

"Record," she said.

Jamuka translated for Fred. The men talked fast

in Mongolian, waving their arms around in heated discussion. Unable to rely on Fizz with his depleted energy reserves, Nat handwrote as quickly as she could, trying hard not to miss any detail: two older members of the Clan were already dead and the list of names of the sick grew by the day. Symptoms mounted up – vomiting, headache, dizziness, diarrhoea, high temperature, flushed cheeks, stomach ache, bloodshot eyes, trembles, deafness, earache, joint ache, persistent coughing.

"Give me details of your diet. I need to know every ingredient of every dish; leave nothing out," continued Fred.

Mutton, goat, goat's milk, horse milk, flour, butter, rice. Nat wondered if they ever ate a vegetable.

"Where have you been? Have you seen signs of anything unusual?"

And so the questions went on. Finally, when at last Fred was satisfied that every piece of relevant information had been extracted, she dismissed them. A shot of pain ran through Nat's fingers where they'd been cramped around the pencil.

"Your thoughts?" asked Jamuka when the villagers had left.

Fred inhaled deeply. Nat clapped her hands over

her ears in anticipation.

"I need to te…eee…eee…sst," she sang, climbing up through an octave.

Jamuka waited for her to finish. "Please let me know if you need anything to aid you."

Fred pursed her lips. "Tea, plenty of it, please. Then we shall start, eh, assistant?"

Nat inwardly groaned. Life under Fred's orders was about to get worse.

Chapter Fifty-Three
CLOSER

The slope was steeper than he thought. Burilgi started to slip, unable to grip the ice. With him came a mini avalanche as he barrelled down. A tree in his path finally broke his fall. He lay there for a moment, breathless and exhausted. It had been a long while since he'd exerted himself like this. Life in Barzurka revolved around bars, shady business deals, eating bowls of gheep stew and drinking vodka. This was more exercise than he'd taken all year.

Rolling over, he could now see all the way down the valley. The snowfall had stopped and a thin sliver of moon had broken through. With his one good eye, he could make out the clearing in the distance where the Clan's camp lay. Someone was shouting. He could hear them but not clearly enough to understand what they were saying. It was only when he heard an all-too-familiar roar that he realised who it was. Despite the cold his palms started to moisten, the sour taste of hate bubbling up and filling his mouth.

His father was still alive. The poison had not reached him yet. *Ugui*.

Chapter Fifty-Four
SECRET OF THE CLAN

Jamuka boiled up a fresh batch of salty tea.

"I think it is time that I told you the secret of the Clan, Bao Bao."

"Secret?" said Nat from where she was lying next to the stove and propping her sleepy head up on her elbow.

"The Clan, all except Buqa – but he is not Clan since he only married into it – has agreed that we should reveal it to you."

"What kind of secret?"

"One upon which I must ask you to swear an oath."

"A promise?"

He handed her a small bowl of *airag* and opened the stove door. "Indeed. Now, throw this in to make your pledge."

Nat tossed the contents into the flames. They hissed, turning a scorched blue. She was now fully awake.

"Once you hear the secret, you are as much its guardian as we are."

Nat slipped her hand into her pocket and touched Fizz's snout to record.

"As you know, our Clan has roamed the Steppe and these mountains for many tens of generations. A thousand years ago a member of our Clan, a medicine man named Jelme, created something that helped change the world order. He used plants to create cures for sickness. He would travel far and wide across the Steppe searching for new supplies and specimens.

"One day he discovered a new plant in a summer pasture. It had the most beautiful deep-red petals. He took samples to run tests upon but every time he cut into a petal it instantly withered and died. He was about to give up, when he tried cutting one of the petals in a different way and it began to ooze a blood-red liquid. He captured the droplets and carried out some experiments.

"Nothing happened until he mixed a drop with the sap of a lumen tree. The mixture frothed and turned from bright red to dark purple. When the final bubble burst, Jelme took a sip.

"All of a sudden he felt an enormous surge of energy. His veins started to pulse with an increased flow of blood. He sprinted out of his *ger*, out on to the Steppe.

CRIMSON POISON

"His horse saw him and came to trot alongside, but Jelme accelerated. Soon they were running neck and neck, the horse at a flat-out gallop."

"No one can run that fast!" said Nat.

Jamuka handed her a bowl of salty tea.

"Finally his horse collapsed, exhausted," he continued. "But Jelme's energy knew no bounds. He carried his horse back to camp on his shoulders. The ones who saw him said he showed the strength of twenty men.

"But just as he entered the camp he collapsed to the ground, all his strength drained away. He had to be carried to his *ger*, where he lay, unable to move or speak, for a week."

"Was the plant Tumen Vachir?" asked Nat.

Jamuka held up his hand. "There's more, Bao Bao. At the end of that week Jelme was able to sit up and, little by little, he could walk again. All that time the dark-purple mixture called to him. One night, unable to resist it any longer, he filled an entire cup and gulped it down."

Chapter Fifty-Five
TEMUJIN

Jamuka poured another bowlful of salty tea and took a loud slurp. Nat sat wide-eyed, gripped by the story.

"This time Jelme ran so fast that time seemed to stand still. The Clan watched him wrestle a line-up of the strongest men. He defeated them one after another. The liquid's effects lasted longer than before. It was not until late the next day that he finally collapsed.

"As he lay in his *ger*, a young hunter entered. His name was Temujin. Temujin was curious to know more. Jelme still could not speak, so Temujin dismissed the young girl who cared for him and stayed to care for Jelme himself.

"Eventually, as his voice returned, Jelme shared the secret of the potion.

"On the promise that he would give them a large share of the bounty, Temujin persuaded some of the Clan to take the potion and make a surprise raid on a neighbouring tribe. They would, he assured them, have more than enough horses, goats and sheep never to have to fight again.

"These men fought the battle with their new strength and speed, and quickly overcame the enemy. Those who were captured in turn pledged allegiance to Temujin. The alternative was death. He used this tactic again and again, soon conquering the Steppe. He became Genghis Khan and the plant that helped him was Tumen Vachir."

He stopped. Nat looked up at him.

"Is this another of your Clan fairytales?" she said.

He shook his head. "Sadly not, Bao Bao. Genghis Khan made everyone in the Clan pledge an oath to keep the secret of the tonic, which he named Tumen Vachir, after the plant. The penalty for disclosing the secret was a swift and merciless death."

Nat shuddered at the thought. "So when did the Clan stop using the potion?"

"Just before he died, Genghis Khan commanded that Tumen Vachir no longer be used. He had by then conquered much of the known world. He wished for his people to live in peace and have their strength intact to give them the energy to keep his kingdom intact. On the day he died the last of the supplies were destroyed and the tonic was never made again.

"But he also instructed the Clan to swear an oath

to pass on the secret to future generations, in case there should ever be a situation that called for Tumen Vachir. That was a thousand years ago. Since then our Clan has grown and spread throughout the whole of Mongolia, keeping the secret with it all this time."

There was a sudden gasp from behind the curtain. Jamuka leapt to his feet and rushed over. Nat followed.

Nat let out a loud shriek. Aunt Tolui's eyes were bulging out of their sockets. Blood was trickling from the corner of her mouth.

Jamuka put his hand gently to his aunt's neck, searching for her pulse.

"Please. Allow me," said Fred, rushing in through the door.

He moved to one side for Fred. He put his hand on Nat's shoulder, the sadness in his eyes making tears spring up in her own.

"It's a terrible business, this Marbolic," said Fred, straightening up.

Nat saw that she had closed Aunt Tolui's eyes and wiped away the blood. Jamuka bowed forward, planting a light kiss on her forehead.

"Farewell, Aunt. I give my word I will hunt out who did this, and make them pay."

Chapter Fifty-Six
ARROW

It was as if time had stood still in the valley. The camp looked exactly the same as it had done when he was a boy. It remained nestled in the clearing at the bottom of the mountain. Having vowed never to return, here he was. The smell of smoke hung in the air. The taste of bile rose in his mouth, making him want to retch.

He crept closer, surprised that one of the wolves hadn't spotted him yet. Maybe they'd all died from Marbolic poisoning. He hoped so. He had hoped to get there and find the whole Clan and wolf pack dead but evidently some were still alive, including his father.

His hand flew up to his eyepatch, covering it with his glove, trying to block out the memory of the hunting trip with his father, a wretched drunk. A flash of pain shot through him at the memory of the agony caused by the arrow as it shot through the air and pierced his eyeball.

He had learned to hate from an early age.

Raised voices from down in the camp dragged him back to the present. A wolf began to howl. One of the *ger* doors sprang open and to his surprise a tall girl with long red hair came flying out shouting, "Help!" in English. Who was she? What was she doing there?

He watched as two men emerged from another *ger*, and came to her aid. Muffled voices, and then the chanting began, accompanied by a lone wolf's howl.

A satisfied smile spread across his face. Another villager dead, and there looked to be only a handful left to deal with.

He took out a bottle of *airag* from his pocket and pulled out the cork. Toasting himself, he took a long swig. Despite the cold, beads of sweat formed on his forehead. He felt power return to him. He just had to find a way to make sure none of them lived. Perhaps he'd been too easy on them, letting the poison seep slowly downstream and into their water supply. He had to find a quicker way to kill them, something much more efficient. He wanted to wipe the Clan out once and for all.

Chapter Fifty-Seven
NEWS

The General smoothed his hair down with a big meaty hand. The American news reporter for CQN pushed the microphone in close.

"So, let me get this clear. The Barzurkan army has a new secret biological weapon, which will change the world order."

"That is correct," he said.

"But you haven't told us what it is, where it is or how it will manifest itself."

"Correct."

"So how do we know you're telling the truth? Perhaps it is merely a mythical weapon?"

The General puffed out his chest.

"We Barzurkans do not make mythical weapons."

"So when will you reveal it?"

"I like to think of it as more of an unveiling."

He pulled a fat cigar out of his pocket. His aide leaned in with a lighter. The General took a drag and blew a huge cloud of blue smoke right at the camera lens.

"Tomorrow. Come back to my headquarters tomorrow and all will be revealed."

Chapter Fifty-Eight
PAPER HORSES

Nat was in a deep sleep when Jamuka woke her. The wood had burned low in the stove, the embers bathing everything in an orange glow.

"Get up and come with me, Bao Bao. We must get up to the mountaintop before sunrise," he said.

"What?"

He held up a bag.

"We must send a message."

"With a bag?"

He smiled. "I will show you. Come."

He offered his hand. She took it and clambered to her feet.

"Wear two coats," he said, holding them up.

When she stepped outside into the freezing, dark night, she understood why. The cold was bone-bitingly deep even in two thick layers of wool.

Her horse was standing ready and waiting next to Jamuka's. Jebe stood, his golden eyes glowing in the dark.

"I'll help you up," said Jamuka.

She placed her boot in his cupped hand. He boosted her up into the saddle, then handed her a flask.

"*Ma huang* tea to help you against the cold. Drink it, then we ride fast," he said, springing up on to his horse.

He softly clicked his horse on.

"Where are we going?" said Nat.

"To a sacred mountaintop. After, we will head north to an area the Clan has not yet searched."

By the time they reached the summit, the first glimmer of dawn was creeping into the dark night. Nat stiffly dismounted, the frozen snow crunching under her boots. Her hands were cramped from holding the reins. She flexed and banged her gloves together to get the circulation flowing again. When she exhaled, her breath crystallised in puffs of white.

Jamuka took off his backpack and set it down on a slab of black rock. Reaching inside, he brought out the brown cloth bag.

"We are ready," he said, climbing up on to the rock.

Nat joined him; Jebe followed. The fear she had felt earlier melted away as they stood side by side on top of the rock. It was like standing on top of the world.

CRIMSON POISON

Fingers of rose-tinted light were creeping across the white-covered plains of the Steppe below. Nat felt as if they were the only humans left on earth.

"It is time to call upon the spirits to come to our aid, Bao Bao," said Jamuka, passing her the bag. "Open it and let the wind do the rest."

He started to chant from the base of his throat, like a gurgling mountain stream. Jebe lifted his head and let out a long mournful howl.

Nat removed her glove, reached into the bag and pulled out a handful of paper horses, cut from an old notebook. They fluttered up into the air like butterflies and drifted off into the brilliant dawn.

Jamuka's chanting reached a crescendo as the final horse moved out of sight. Jebe let out one long last howl. Their voices trailed off, leaving a whispering quiet.

They sat down cross-legged on the ground, eyes closed in meditation. Nat focused her thoughts and prayers towards the journey of the paper horses.

A wet nose pressed into her face. She opened her eyes to see Jebe staring at her. He whined and then walked over to the other side of the mountain. He looked back at her and whined again.

"What is it?" she said.

Chapter Fifty-Nine
MRS McTAVISH

"Henry, come to the sunroom, please. I have someone I'd like you to meet," said Aunt Vera, calling him through NutNut's intercom.

Henry sighed and closed the Mongolian history book he had been reading. He wanted to be with Nat, and not at his mother's beck and call as she went into "spending overdrive", as his father called it. Deliveries of new clothes, sample furnishings and fabrics had been arriving round the clock. Only the night before, the whole household had been woken up by a late-night delivery of marble, flown over from Italy.

It was probably another designer or architect she wanted to parade him in front of. He trudged along the hallway, taking his time.

Instead, he was surprised to find a white-haired woman in a red kilt, brown stockings and lace-up brown shoes scowling at him. She eyed him up as if he was a specimen under a microscope.

"Henry darling, please meet Mrs McTavish," said his mother.

He walked up and held out his hand. "Hello."

Mrs McTavish's hand was cold and bony. "A nice firm handshake, young man. You've done well with the manners, Mrs Walker. That'll make my job so much easier."

"Job?" said Henry.

"Come and sit here," said his mother, patting the yellow sofa.

Mrs McTavish was keeping a beady eye on him. He smelled a rat, a large rat.

"Now that we're going to have a bigger family, not to mention a bigger house and a very busy new social life, I need help, so Mrs McTavish has kindly flown in from Scotland to be your new nanny."

"Nanny?" said Henry, jumping up. "I don't need a nanny!"

"Not just for you. It's for the Brat – I mean Natalie – as well."

"What about Prissy?"

"She's old enough to look after herself."

"No." Henry stamped his foot, his blood boiling.

"I'll soon put a stop to *this* sort of behaviour," said Mrs McTavish, raising a bushy eyebrow.

"Mrs McTavish comes from your ancestors' old hometown of Loch Tavish. I've long considered it important that you should have some influence from the old country."

"I don't need her or my old country," said Henry, gritting his teeth.

Aunt Vera checked her watch. "Look at the time, so much to do. Now, I must dash to my next meeting. I'll leave you two to get acquainted."

"Please, Mummy, no!" said Henry, grabbing on to her arm. "I'll come with you."

Mrs McTavish stepped forward and, with a surprising show of strength, she prised Henry's fingers off his mother's arm. "We'll have none of that, Henry. You need to show your mother the respect she deserves."

Aunt Vera slipped out of the door without another word, leaving him stranded. Mrs McTavish leaned in close to his face. Her breath smelled fishy.

"Now then, Henry Walker, let me tell you my list of rules."

Chapter Sixty
AMBUSH

Jebe was racing down the side of the mountain.

"Wait!" called Nat, glancing back at Jamuka, but she could see that he was in a deep meditation. He would remain like that for an hour, at least.

Jebe stopped his descent and whined again, urging her to follow him. She did a quick calculation – if they were quick she could be back before Jamuka emerged from his meditation.

She took off after him. He waited for her to catch up. The mountainside was so steep that she almost lost her footing. She reached him and clung on for support.

They quickly reached a line of fir trees. Jebe's nose went to the ground. He took off at a lope, on a scent. Nat broke into a jog to keep up.

Just when she thought she couldn't run any further Jebe halted up ahead. She caught up with him. He was standing beside a mountain stream, sniffing some fresh tracks in the snow.

Bending down to take a closer look she realised that they were not made by a forest animal. They were long thin slices, cut by a pair of skis. A feeling of unease settled on her. Maybe she should have waited for Jamuka.

Jebe began to paw the ground, his tail twitching.

"What?"

He took off at a run.

"Wait," she said, following him.

They came around a bend in the bank. Up ahead stood a waterfall where two men were busy emptying containers of crimson liquid into the stream. A foul stench of rotten eggs hit Nat's nostrils. One of the men was tall, dressed in a military uniform, while the other was short and squat.

Jebe growled. Before she could stop him, he leapt across the bank, charging towards them. Quick as a flash the tall man spun round, pulled out a gun and fired. A *CRACK!* split the air. Jebe let out a high-pitched yelp and fell to the ground.

"No!" cried Nat, leaping across to him.

She fell to her knees. Blood was seeping from his side into the white snow.

The man strode over and kicked Jebe.

"Stop it!" screamed Nat.

CRIMSON POISON

She sprang up, kicking high into the air at the man but his hand shot out, blocking her. She turned. Using all her strength, she leapt forward aiming a one-inch punch to his head, adrenalin coursing through her body. But quick as a flash, before her punch met him he clipped her hard on the side of her head with the butt of his revolver. She could feel herself falling backwards. Then everything went black.

Chapter Sixty-One
BIOLOGICAL WEAPON

The CQN reporter and cameraman were led into an empty parade ground for their exclusive interview with the General. An icy Siberian wind was gusting across, bearing snow. Blocks of grey buildings with bars over the windows lined each side of the ground. A red-carpeted podium with a tented roof stood at the centre.

"You can film from here," said the General, greeting them at the steps.

They assembled their equipment and ran a test.

"Ready?" said the General, puffing on a cigar.

The reporter nodded and started the interview. The camera focused in on the General's puffy face. While they spoke a line of uniformed soldiers came marching into the parade ground, a tank rumbling in behind them. The reporter raised her voice to be heard over the din.

"Watch," ordered the General, cutting in on the reporter.

CRIMSON POISON

The camera followed his arm as he waved towards the far corner of the parade ground. Suddenly a dark shadow came rocketing around the corner, heading like a missile at the soldiers.

"What the—" said the reporter, her jaw dropping. "Is that a man?"

The man reached the first soldier and high-kicked him straight across the parade ground. He then chased him like the wind and caught him mid-air, before tossing him at the podium.

The soldier came crashing down on the red carpet, narrowly missing the camera. The man turned and charged at the remaining soldiers, engaging them in hand-to-hand combat. He was a whirlwind of kicks, punches and throws. Screams of agony rang out across the yard. Within seconds he had taken out every one of his opponents, casting them to all four corners of the parade ground.

The reporter was lost for words. She stood rooted to the spot, the microphone frozen in her hand.

The man let out a fierce roar and ran at the tank. He flipped it on to its roof, and continued to flip it along the ground like a rolling stone.

"Enough!" ordered the General.

The man stopped, turned and saluted the General.

The cameraman caught the image that would go worldwide in a viral explosion – a super-soldier wearing black ops gear and a balaclava stamped with Barzurka's heraldic emblem.

"Is that," said the reporter, her voice shaky, "Barzurka's new weapon? How is this possible, General?"

The General smiled. "It is in the Barzurkan blood. We have it in our blood."

Chapter Sixty-Two
MRS McTAVISH

It was late when Mrs McTavish finally gave Henry leave to go to his bedroom.

"*Hai*. I was about to give up on you," said Wen, picking up his call. "Have you seen that crazy Barzurkan General and his bionic soldier on the news?"

Henry shook his head.

"*Wa sai*, it's scary stuff. Everyone's saying it's a hoax, but imagine if it's not? Dad says we'll have Barzurkan super-soldiers invading China before we know it."

"I couldn't get away from the horrible new nanny Mummy's hired."

Wen snorted. "A nanny? You're not a baby!"

"I've had to follow her rules ever since she got here this morning – cold shower, one hour extra maths homework, one hour learning the future perfect – in Latin. And she made me finish a whole bowl of lumpy salt porridge before I could get down from the table. She smells of rotten eggs and she's going to be Nat's nanny too."

"Never!"

"And we went to the new house today. Mummy showed us the new wing they're designing. It's like a prison. They're going to put Nat in there with Mrs McTavish and now Mrs McTavish is saying she'll do a better job of controlling me if I'm in there as well."

"Well, we're going to have to stop them, aren't we?"

"But we can't unless we get Nat back in time."

Wen smiled. "Don't worry. There are still a few days left before it goes to court. If that doesn't work I'll hire one of those Barzurkan super-soldiers to come and sort your nanny out."

Henry's shoulders slumped. He tried to fight back the tears but they came anyway. "I hate my family. They're all horrid. Prissy just ignores me, Daddy is out at his club the whole time and Mummy is busy with her new life. I wish I didn't exist."

"Don't say that." Wen leaned into camera. "We need you, Henry. Nat needs you, and she's a part of your family. So you'd better shape up, ding-a-ling, and we can put together a plan for when she returns."

Chapter Sixty-Three
NORTH

Smoke caught at the back of Nat's throat, making her cough. She tried to move her head but daggers of pain shot up through her skull. Her eyes flickered open. She was lying on a grubby felt pad next to a stove. Smoke was curling up and out of its loose-fitting door, filling the *ger* with a grey haze.

On the other side of the tent she spotted the short, squat man from the waterfall. He was seated at a table, bent over a microscope. Nat tried to move, but found her hands were tied together behind her back and that her feet were bound by rope. She wondered how long she'd been there. Her mouth was dry, her throat parched.

"Water," she croaked.

The man looked up. Her eyes widened in fright. He wore a black patch over one eye. A deep scar ran from his forehead to his neck.

"Quiet!" he barked in thickly accented English.

"Please, I'm thirsty."

He grunted, got to his feet, grabbed a jug from another table and poured its contents into a filthy cup. He limped over and held it roughly to her lips.

"Drink."

Nat took a sip. She spat it out on the mat. Her throat was on fire. The man laughed and returned to his table. Tears welled up. She bit her lip.

"Please let me go."

"Ha," he said. "You rich Hong Kong girl. Now you make me rich."

How could he know about her? Unless...

"You are Clan?"

He banged his fist on the table. "Do not speak to me of Clan!"

Nat squeezed her eyes shut, wishing the nightmare to end. The man was muttering to himself now. Nat hadn't a clue what he was saying until...

"Buqa?" she said, hearing him shout the big angry man's name.

"What?" he roared, spinning round.

She shrank back, curling herself up into a ball as he jumped off his chair and came barrelling across the tent.

"Buqa?" he said, leaning in, jabbing his finger at his eyepatch. "I tell you about Buqa. Look!"

He lifted the patch. She averted her gaze, starting to sob.

"My father is Buqa. He did this. Bad man. Look!" he screamed.

She turned towards him. His stale breath hung in the air between them. Underneath the patch lay a shrivelled, sunken, eyeless socket. He dropped the patch back in place.

"I'm sorry," she whispered.

Her words seemed to calm him. He grunted and stood up.

"We hunted. His arrow. Bam!" he said, putting his hand over the patch.

"I'm very sorry."

He spat on the mat. "Buqa." He spat again.

"Is that why you're poisoning the Clan?" said Nat.

He looked at her, cocking his head to one side.

"Bad people."

"Why?"

"Father bad, I fight him. Clan, and mother, Gan, threw me out. I walk three weeks to Barzurka."

"Please don't kill everyone."

He shrugged. "They must be punished," and strode back to the table where he reached underneath, grabbed a bottle and took a long drink.

Nat felt the bile rise in her stomach. She was way out of her depth but she had to try.

"I am Nat," she said. "What is your name?"

He wiped his lips on his sleeve. "My name Burilgi."

"Burilgi, please. I'm only—"

The door opened. A tall soldier stepped inside, accompanied by another shorter one, both carrying several bushy plants with huge red flowers. Nat's eyes grew wide. Massive Tumen Vachir plants.

The soldiers dumped them on the ground and barked orders at Burilgi. He shouted back at them. Moments later they left without even glancing at her. Nat tried to move her hands but they were bound too tightly. Her head felt as if someone was banging it with a hammer.

Burilgi bent over his table again. He held a test tube full of fizzing purple froth up to the light.

"Please let me go," she tried again.

He put the tube down, got to his feet and strode over, flashing a knife in her face.

"One more word, I cut off your ear," he hissed.

Chapter Sixty-Four
PURSUIT

Altan slowed to a trot and checked his watch. He smiled. His timing was good. Jamuka and Princess would be about ready for them all to head off on their planned search for the Tumen Vachir plants in the north. He was reaching into his saddlebag for his flask of salty tea when three long howls echoed across the valley. His heart quickened. The howls came again. He listened carefully, pinpointing their direction before throwing back his head and answering with two short yelps.

He urged his horse into a gallop. It stretched its neck out, accelerating through the trees. The early morning icy air bit into his cheeks. Branches flashed past as he ducked and dodged. Maybe Prin— Nat had had another asthma attack.

He finally came out of the forest to find a stream across his path. He reined his horse to a stop. The water was dirty and a foul stench hit his nostrils.

"Over here!"

He shaded his eyes against the sun bouncing off the water and looked upstream to find Jamuka crouching over something on the ground.

Altan dismounted and ran over to his uncle. Jamuka was quickly binding Jebe's leg with a torn piece of his coat. Patches of bright-red blood dripped onto the snow beneath. Jebe's golden eyes looked pained.

"Bad?" Altan said.

"Shot," said Jamuka.

"Nat?"

Jamuka got to his feet. His face was ashen.

"It looks like she's been taken."

Altan swallowed hard. "Taken?" he said, the word sticking in his throat.

Jamuka pointed to deep tracks in the snow, leading off up north. He walked over to his horse and jumped up into the saddle.

"We'll need back-up. Get Tabin and Temur, then follow my tracks."

Chapter Sixty-Five
THE WING

It took another jug of *airag* for Burilgi to fall asleep at the table. Nat waited, listening, until his snores reached a constant rhythm. This could well be her only chance. Through the open chimney in the roof she could see the pale light of dawn.

"Fizz," she whispered.

A faint whirring sound came from inside her pocket and his small snout popped up.

"Open wings," she said.

"*Low en ... er ... gy.*" He sounded faint.

"Please."

His eyes blinked. His wings emerged slowly from the pocket. She rolled over, letting him fall out on to the mat. Rolling back the other way, she was able to grab a wing in her hand. She began to rub the sharp edge of the wing against the rope.

"*Stop. Fizz break,*" he protested, trying to retract the wing.

But Nat had it wedged.

"Sorry," she said, close to tears. "OK to break."

The wing began making progress; the rope started to fray. Her hands were tired but she kept going. She was halfway through when the wing snapped off. Fizz's body fell to the mat and shut down.

Nat gritted her teeth and carried on sawing with his broken wing. Just as the rope broke free she felt her breath shorten, her chest tighten. She grabbed Fizz and put him in her pocket. Don't panic. She began to count her breaths, in and out, as she set about loosening the rope around her feet.

The door opened.

Quick as a flash she lay back down. The tall soldier walked in and over to Burilgi. He picked up the empty jug next to him, sniffed it, kicked him and strode out, slamming the door behind him. Burilgi didn't move. He was out cold.

Nat sat up. This time she managed to undo the knots, but already the room was starting to swim, and her *ma huang* tea was with her horse. She couldn't die here.

Altan's face came back to her. He had shown her how to take short breaths during her attack in the forest. She tried to take in tiny wisps of air, but the thick, smoky air made her choke.

CRIMSON POISON

She had to do something… She started crawling across the *ger*. Black spots danced in front of her eyes and her lungs felt as if they were going to burst.

With one last breath she dragged herself up, shakily gripping the table, and reached for the test tubes.

"What the…?" growled Burilgi, his good eye snapping open.

His hand shot out but Nat had already grabbed the test tube of dark-purple liquid, put it to her lips and swallowed.

"No!" he roared, punching her back on to the mat.

A jolt of electricity surged through Nat's body. Her airways opened up. Her lungs became bellows and her eyes popped wide. Her muscles twitched and trembled. In an instant she was on her feet.

Burilgi lunged at her but she spun round, catching his shoulder with a high kick.

"Aaaargh!" he shouted, reeling backwards.

Seeing her opportunity, she ran for the door but he sprang in front of her. She dodged left towards the table. Leaping up into the air, she brought her knees to her chest and somersaulted high over Burilgi's head, coming to land at the door.

She pushed it open and bolted out into the snow,

surprising a couple of soldiers who were drinking vodka from shot glasses. They laughed when they saw her, and formed a human wall, blocking the only exit between the tents.

Nat ran headlong at them. She jumped up off the ground, propelling both legs forward.

Crack!

She hit them squarely in the middle of their foreheads with her feet so fast that they didn't have time to react. She tumbled over the top of them, bounced up off the ground and took off, running like the wind.

She emerged into a compound surrounded by high wire fencing. A row of polytunnel greenhouses lined one side, a snow-white field was on the other.

Unsure of where to go, with a new set of guards hot on her heels, Nat started to run downhill towards the far end of the compound.

A bullet whistled past her ear. She willed herself to go faster.

A volley of shouts echoed across the compound. The gunfire stopped. She became aware of someone closing in behind her. Glancing over her shoulder, she saw that it was Burilgi.

She was nearly at the fence. With another surge of energy she leapt up, flying through the air towards its chain links. Her hands gripped on to them like a monkey.

Suddenly the fence shook with a terrible force. Someone grabbed her ankle, her hands were torn away and she fell.

Chapter Sixty-Six
FIGHT

Burilgi put his knee on Nat's chest and clamped his hands around her neck.

"Die!" he said, tightening his grip.

A black shadow flew through the air, knocking Burilgi off his feet. A huge wolf clamped its jaws firmly around the back of the man's neck.

"Jebe!" Nat cried.

But Burilgi wrenched the wolf off him. Jebe howled in pain, landing with a thud in the snow. Once again, Burilgi lunged at Nat. This time she was ready. She popped a one-inch punch at his head. The force knocked him sideways to the ground.

"Catch, Princess!" came a shout.

Nat looked up to see Altan throwing her the end of a metal-mesh net. She caught the edge and as Burilgi staggered back to his feet, they threw the net over him, trapping him like a bear. He tried to fight it off but Nat ran lightning-fast circles around him, winding the net ever tighter until he was completely caught, his arms pinned to his sides. Altan pushed him over on to the ground and padlocked the net together.

Nat threw her arms around Altan in relief.

"Easy, Princess," he said, almost crushed by her strength.

She let go. "Sorry."

Jebe pushed his nose under her hand.

"I thought you were dead," she said, rubbing his chest.

A loud explosion boomed out from the other end of the compound. She turned to see that the greenhouses were alight. Smoke and shouting filled the air.

"The others?" she said, looking at Altan before sprinting up the field with Jebe at her side.

She reached the *ger* tents to find four soldiers tied together in the centre of the camp. Tabin was standing over them, his coat streaked with blood. A cry came from one of the tents. Nat rushed inside to find Temur and Jamuka engaged in fierce kung fu fighting with three soldiers in their underwear. Mattresses and sleeping bags were strewn across the floor.

Without hesitation, Nat leapt into the air and flew across the *ger* at one of the soldiers. Her boot met his shoulder with a *CRACK!*

"*Aiiiiiii!*" he cried.

Immediately Jebe leapt on top of him and pinned him to the ground.

The soldier who was fighting Temur spun round and his leg flew out to kick her. But Nat saw it coming and reached out, grabbed it and twisted. Hard. *SNAP!*

"Urgh!" the soldier cried, slumping to the ground.

Nat chopped him at the neck.

He passed out.

Jamuka whirled round, lifting his leg high, but the last soldier was clearly a black belt. He deflected the move and came at Jamuka with a right chop. Nat predicted the move before it happened. Just as he was going to hit Jamuka's cheek, she leapt forward, bringing her hand into a tiger claw and grabbing the soldier's shoulder. *POP!* She dislocated it.

"Eurgh!" he screamed.

Jamuka punched him in the stomach and he collapsed on to the ground.

"Quick, tie them up," he said, tossing her a coil of rope.

Fizzing with energy, Nat grabbed the rope, uncoiled it in one whip of her hand and before the others could help, she had wound it around the soldiers.

Jamuka hugged her tight, then released her. "You must run as fast as you can to Altan, Bao Bao.

You don't have much time. Be swift, like the wind. Go!"

She turned and ran outside. Jebe followed. They bounded back down to where Altan was waiting, with Burilgi.

She threw Burilgi over her shoulder like a sack of potatoes.

"You crazy strong, Princess," said Altan.

"Not for long. It's about to wear off and then you'll have to carry us both."

Altan took her hand, leading her to a hole that had been cut in the fence.

She tossed Burilgi over the fence and caught him the other side.

"Down," said Altan, pointing through the forest.

She took off at a sprint with Jebe at her side.

A familiar whinny up ahead spurred her on. She reached her horse and threw Burilgi across the saddle.

"Take him," she shouted back to Altan.

"You?" he said, catching up, breathless.

"I have to run," she said, her heart beating fast, the blood pumping through her veins.

"Follow Jebe," he said.

Nat followed the black wolf at top speed. She'd never felt so alert, so alive.

Jebe slowed to a lope at the bottom of the valley. Nat could now hear the unmistakable sound of Fred's warble. They came to a small clearing where Fred sat astride her carthorse, holding a large test tube in her gloved hand.

"You're alive!" sang Fred at the top of her voice.

She jumped down from the saddle and gave Nat a big slap on the back.

"Have they retrieved any Tumen Vachir yet? I'm here on standby, following orders."

Nat shook her head. All of a sudden her whole body started to tremble. It was as if someone had pulled the plug. All her energy drained away. Her knees buckled. She fell to the ground.

"Now's not the time for theatrics," said Fred.

"I took some," whispered Nat, her voice now a faint whisper.

Jebe whined and started to lick her face. Fred shoved his nose out of the way.

"Are you poisoned?"

"No," said Altan, thundering up on his horse. He had Nat's in tow carrying a strapped-down Burilgi.

He jumped down. "She take secret."

"What *are* you talking about?" said Fred.

Chapter Sixty-Seven
COMA

The drumming of horses' hooves pounded through Nat's ears, tattooing her mind with their rhythm. Using every drop of energy she could muster, she half opened her eyes to find Jamuka's head looming over her. His eyes were screwed tight against the biting wind, his hat pulled down low, the fur flaps anchored down over his ears. He was focused on the path ahead, beyond where she lay cradled in his arms. She had no idea how long she had been asleep or where they were. Her eyelids started to droop. When she tried to form words, nothing came out. Every muscle in her body was limp.

What if she stayed like this forever?

This question played in her mind, over and over, until she passed out again, into a coma-like sleep.

Chapter Sixty-Eight
RECKONING

The General stood amid the smoking ashes of the camp.

"You imbeciles!" he roared at the injured soldiers. "You're telling me that a red-haired girl, a wolf and some ragtag group of Mongolian nomads did this?"

No one spoke. No one uttered a word.

He smashed a half-full bottle of vodka over the nearest soldier's head. The soldier screamed.

"You're a bunch of snivelling drunks. I should never have given you such an allowance. One of you probably fell drunk over your stove and set the camp on fire. You burned that Mongolian too, eh?"

He spat on the ground, then looked into the terrified eyes of the soldiers, searching for answers.

"Take them back to headquarters on foot. Then torture them until you find the truth," he ordered the soldiers who he'd brought with him.

He tossed his cigar into the ashes and turned to his waiting Speedcopter.

Chapter Sixty-Nine
GAN

The "laaaaaaa" of Fred hitting a top note woke her. She found herself looking up at the stained canvas roof of Tolui's old *ger* tent. Smoke curled upwards from the stove creating hazy patterns in the lamplight. A warm nose nudged her hand. Very slowly she moved her head to find Jebe staring at her.

"This is confounded!" sang Fred. She held a test tube in one hand, out of which poured yellow smoke. "My assumptions are wrong!"

Fred rammed the test tube back into a rack, pushed back the chair, got to her feet and turned towards the stove. Even with her taped-together glasses perched on her nose, Nat could see how bloodshot her eyes were.

"Aha, you are awake," sang Fred.

Nat managed a weak smile. Fred thrust a hand in her coat pocket. She pulled out a small brown bottle and knelt down next to her.

"I can't find an antidote to this wretched poison but

I can at least cure you. Drink," she said, putting her hand under Nat's head to bring her up to the edge of the bottle. The smell made Nat's eyes water.

"Open your mouth," said Fred.

Nat did as she was told. Fred poured in a spoonful. A bitter, spicy taste filled her mouth. Yuk. Closing her eyes, she forced herself to swallow the foul-tasting liquid.

"Good," said Fred. "Give it a couple of hours and you'll be as right as rain."

"Water?" croaked Nat.

Fred shook her head.

"Absolutely not. We need it full strength, no dilution," she said, getting back to her feet.

"What about the antidote?" croaked Nat.

Fred spread her arms and opened her mouth wide. Nat winced in anticipation.

"It is a trial. My mixtures and my methods are in vain," blasted Fred, singing at the top of her voice. "What can I do?"

The door sprang open and Jamuka came in, his look of concern giving way to a broad smile.

"Bao Bao," he said, falling to his knees, enveloping her in a large hug. "You are back with us."

He sat back and took her hand in his. "I am sorry to

have put you in such danger."

Fred grabbed her hat. "I'm off out for more raw materials," she announced, striding towards the door.

"The others?" Nat whispered when she was gone.

Jamuka paused. His eyes were ringed with dark shadows.

"We all made it back but Gan is dead."

"Gan?" she said. "Burilgi's mother?"

"Yes, Gan died before we had brought Burilgi back to the camp. It was probably best she did not see her disgraced son. He drank the rest of the elixir that he'd made in his tent so that he could chase and stop you. It was a huge amount, far greater than what you had taken. It is doubtful he will ever walk again so it now falls to Buqa to care for him."

"He killed his mother," said Nat, a chill running through her.

Jamuka nodded.

"Burilgi has admitted to selling the Tumen Vachir to the Barzurkan army. He wanted to make himself a fortune."

"Have they got some?"

"Not any more. We are lucky that he only gave General Golkova a small vial, which the General used up in a test."

"*Zoinks!* That is lucky," said Nat.

"Indeed, because Fred has discovered that the Growemup fertiliser made the Tumen Vachir into a far more powerful weapon than in Genghis Khan's day. It changed the plant's chemical make-up, amplifying its strength tenfold."

Nat winced. "Did any plants survive?"

Jamuka shook his head. "The Clan's secret remains safe."

"And what about that stuff Burilgi was pouring into the river... Was it Marbolic?"

"Yes. Marbolic, the deadly crimson poison. Burilgi wanted to kill the whole Clan so he made sure that it was taken daily to our river water supply and poured in. We are using another water source now, which Fred has declared safe."

Jebe shifted, lifting his head up to rest on her chest. Nat felt her eyelids start to close. As much as she wanted to stay awake her body cried out for sleep. Jamuka put his hand to her forehead.

"Rest up, Bao Bao. I should go and help Fred."

He put more wood in the stove and headed out into the night.

Nat awoke to the sound of the wind howling outside.

CRIMSON POISON

She was alone, except for Jebe. Turning her head towards the door she saw a newly made wooden box lying next to her pillow. Very slowly, inching her way, she managed to reach its lid. Using her thumb and forefinger, she made a pincer-like movement to grasp it. She failed. Her hand flopped down uselessly on the top.

Jebe lifted his head off his paws. With his nose, he raised her arm, bringing it to rest on the ground. He then put his nose under the edge of the lid, pushing upwards. It popped open.

"Thank you," she whispered.

He rested his head back on his paws, watching her. Little by little she managed to lift her hand, bringing it to rest on the piece of felt that lay inside. The moment her hand touched it she knew what lay underneath. Very slowly, she managed to drag back the cloth.

Fizz's small emerald head peeped out. He was cold to the touch, his eyes closed. The wing she had broken off lay at his side.

Chapter Seventy
TA-DA

"Wake up!"

Nat opened her eyes to see Altan holding up her boots.

"We go now, Princess."

"Where?" she croaked.

"Fast."

He didn't wait for her response. He reached down, lifted her arm out from underneath the blanket and pulled.

Like a puppet on strings she came to her feet. A wave of dizziness washed over her and the room started to spin, but just as she was about to collapse back Altan put her arm around his shoulders to prop her up.

"I can't," she said.

"Fred say you good now. Boot one," he said, dropping it on the floor.

She lifted her leg. It trembled with the effort but she was amazed to find she could move and place it in the boot.

"Next," he said, dropping the other one.

No sooner was she booted than he was sticking her hat on her head, helping her to pull on her coat and her gloves, and hurrying her to the door.

They stepped out into bright sunlight. Nat put her hands up to shield her eyes from the glare. The wind slapped her cheeks. Everywhere was quiet, deathly quiet, until Altan let out a low whistle, and a familiar whinny broke out across the camp.

Her horse came walking between the *gers*. The moment it spotted her, it broke into a trot. Altan caught its reins. It bent its head and started to nuzzle Nat, searching for a snack, but he moved its head to one side so that she could reach the stirrup.

"Up," he said.

"Where are we going?"

She tried to lift her leg but it started to tremble violently. He sighed and cupped his hands.

"Knee."

Altan propelled her up with such force that she nearly shot over the other side. Her horse started to move off.

"Whoa!" she said, fumbling for the reins.

Altan placed them in her gloved hands. She grasped

on to them with what little strength she had.

He put his lips together and let out another whistle. Nat frowned.

"That's Temur's call," she said.

Sure enough, Temur's brown mare appeared from the other side of Tolui's *ger*. Altan jumped up into the saddle.

"Where's your horse?" she asked.

"With ancestors."

He clicked the mare on and it moved off with Nat's horse in its wake. A lump rose in her throat. Altan had loved his horse. He'd told her how they had grown up together, lifelong companions, a Mongolian tradition. Urging her horse forward, she drew up alongside him.

"How did he die?" she said.

Altan stared straight ahead.

"Heart stopped after too much gallop."

"I'm sorry," she said. "He was a brave horse."

Altan kicked Temur's horse into a trot. Nat took a deep breath and spurred hers on. They passed into the thick forest.

The trotting was exhausting. Up, down, down, up. Nat's legs were like jelly so she gripped tight on to the mane, willing herself not to fall off.

Out of the corner of her eye she caught sight of a

dark shadow darting through the trees at top speed. Seconds later, Jebe appeared. He drew up next to her, slowing to a lope.

Up ahead, she could now make out a familiar bulky figure seated on a large rock. At the sound of their approach Fred turned towards them. She was using a long stick to break up ice covering the stream next to her.

"Well, that took some time. I was worried you weren't coming back."

"Sorry," said Altan, jumping down.

Fred stood up and walked over to Nat's horse, offering her a hand down.

Nat swung her leg out of the saddle. Fred caught her.

"Right, let's get to work," she said, helping Nat over to the rock.

A long rack of test tubes, glass bottles, a needle and a surgical steel tray lay on a camp table next to her.

"What's this for?"

"Once I've got the water from the stream, I will take your blood," said Fred.

Nat quivered. "Blood?"

"Because," said Fred, lowering a glass bottle on a string into the stream, "I may be a first-rate botanist and biochemist, but my theories on this confounded Marbolic have so far proven incorrect, so we must pursue this new avenue. Your blood has been exposed to the extremely potent elixir of Tumen Vachir. I believe that, in conjunction with my medicine, it can help formulate a cure for the Marbolic poisoning."

Nat swallowed hard. She looked across at where the enormous syringe, with its glistening needle, lay on the table. She felt sick.

A crackling noise behind made her jump. She turned to see Altan fanning the flames of a neat pile of burning twigs.

Nat watched as Fred pulled the bottle from the stream, set it down on the rock and picked up the syringe. She looked up at Nat, her shaggy grey hair rigid with frost, her round glasses steamed up. Nat shrank back. Jebe let out a low growl.

Chapter Seventy-One
BLOOD

"Wolf, stay down!" shouted Fred, pointing the needle towards him.

Jebe lowered his head, digging his paws into the snow ready to pounce. He let out a deep growl. Altan sprang forward between Jebe and Fred. He crouched down to look Jebe directly in the eyes. Jebe whined and sat down.

Altan placed his hand on Nat's shoulder. She looked up at him. She was trembling from head to toe.

"I can't do this."

"Must, Princess."

The look of desperation in his eyes made her heart sink.

"Right. Coat off. Let's be practical and get on with it," said Fred.

Nat felt like a trapped animal.

"Now?"

"Yes. I shall refer to this as my elixir; that's the proper alchemist's term."

"But alchemists aren't real, are they?" said Nat.

Fred pointed the syringe at her. "They are now."

Nat reached up to undo the buttons of her coat, but her hands were shaking uncontrollably.

Altan reached under her neck for the top button, his warm hands grazing the skin under her chin.

"Chop-chop," said Fred.

He helped her out of her coat. She shivered as the cold wrapped its icy tentacles around her.

"Sleeve up." Fred moved in closer.

Altan took her hand and pushed the wool sleeve up above her elbow. Nat's teeth began to chatter. Fred produced a piece of string from her hat, reached down and wrapped it around Nat's upper arm, pulling it tight.

"Ouch!" said Nat as it pinched in. She buried her free hand in Jebe's black fur.

"We need the pressure," said Fred, holding up the syringe.

Nat gulped. "Is the needle clean?"

"Hmm, good point." Fred reached into her pocket, brought out a bottle and removed the cap.

"*Airag*?" said Altan, sniffing the air.

"I ran out of surgical alcohol a while ago," said Fred, dipping the needle into the bottle. "This will do the trick."

Nat looked at Altan.

"Right," said Fred, taking hold of Nat's arm. She poured the rest of the *airag* over the skin. The fumes made Nat's eyes water.

"Arm sterilised. Needle sterilised," she said, leaning in close. "I spy a good vein here!" she sang.

She drove the needle into Nat's arm.

"Argggghhhhh!" cried Nat.

"Steady!" said Fred.

Altan took hold of Nat's shoulders while Fred released the string. Nat looked down to see her bright-red blood fill the syringe. Her head spun; Fred started to sing: "I see the life force coming from within!"

Chapter Seventy-Two
HOAX

The reporter and cameraman walked into their station editor's office. They'd both been expecting this – the pat-on-the-back, "great job, you both deserve a raise" meeting for the piece they'd done on the General. It was still making world headlines, even now, days after its release.

They were surprised to find the head of human resources and the station's security chief in the office as well. No one was looking in a celebratory mood.

"Take a seat," said the editor, directing them to a pair of chairs set up opposite the committee.

"This is a formal meeting, which is being recorded," began the human resources director.

"What's going on?" said the reporter.

"We've been passed details from the Barzurkan army about the bribe you both took to broadcast their elaborate hoax," said the security chief.

"What?" said the reporter and cameraman, jumping up out of their chairs in unison.

CRIMSON POISON

"The two-hundred-and-fifty-thousand-US-dollar-apiece bribe that is now sitting in bank accounts in your names in Novorovo Bank," said the security chief.

"There was no bribe. The whole super-soldier thing was real. We saw it with our own eyes. I filmed it," said the cameraman.

"That film was a hoax, made by the Barzurkan using the latest CG techniques. You took the money and made us look like fools," said the editor, his face red with fury.

"We didn't. We took nothing. It was real!" said the reporter, jumping to her feet. "As real as this meeting is now, as this building stands!"

"Fools! The moment this gets out our reputation is going to be in shreds!" The editor slammed his hand down hard on his desk.

"But it was real! They have a super-soldier! I'd stake my life on it," said the cameraman.

"Well, you've staked your job on it, you greedy idiot. You're both fired!"

Chapter Seventy-Three
ANTIDOTE

Nat could hear women's laughter, a child giggling and the low rumble of conversation. Her eyes flickered open. She was lying on her back. For a moment she thought she was dreaming. Her last memory was of Fred and her giant needle.

"Princess," said Altan.

Suddenly a cheer went up. She moved her gaze from the ceiling to find the *ger* packed with smiling faces. Temur, Tabin, Fred, Jamuka, along with a crowd of other Clan members she hadn't seen before.

Jamuka stepped across to her side.

"Thanks to you, Fred was able to make an antidote," he said, his brown eyes shining.

"From my blood?"

"Strange as it may sound," said Fred, chewing on a piece of *aaruul*. "Sorry I had to take so much but it did the job."

Nat's arm was throbbing.

"It hurts," she said.

"It's a good job you passed out. I had a devil of a time drawing it out of you," said Fred.

Jamuka put a bowl to her lips. "You need to rebuild your strength."

She took a sip, the warm taste of boiled mutton filling her mouth. "How long have I been asleep?"

"All afternoon," said Jamuka. "Jebe has not left your side."

She reached over and buried her fingers in the wolf's thick fur. He looked up, moving his head to come to a rest in her lap.

Temur stood up. He was holding a bow and an instrument that looked like some sort of violin. He drew the bow across the strings. A screeching moan erupted through the tent. Nat gritted her teeth. He opened his mouth. A deep, gravelly gurgle rose from his throat.

Not to be outdone Fred leapt to her feet, flung her arms wide and released an ear-splitting operatic high-note. The Clan gasped in horror, hands flying to their mouths. A child screamed but it didn't stop Fred, who was now climbing up through an octave.

Temur frowned. He started furiously sawing at the strings with his bow. The gurgling from his throat became a deep rumble of thunder.

Without missing a beat, Fred hit another top note. Jebe threw back his head and began to howl. The noise was cacophonous, deafening and unexpectedly uplifting.

Nat felt a giggle burbling up in her throat. She caught Altan's eye and the two of them burst into fits of laughter.

Chapter Seventy-Four
RETURN

Later that night, after the last of the partygoers had left, Jamuka rolled out his mattress. The fire in the stove had burned low, casting a soft orange glow across the *ger*.

Nat lay on her bed with Jebe at her side.

"We must leave for home early tomorrow, Bao Bao," said Jamuka.

Hong Kong? Nat sat bolt upright. She'd been so immersed in everything here she'd almost forgotten what was waiting for her back there.

"*Zoinks!* We've still got to stop Aunt Vera!" she said, her mind filling with images of Wetley Towers, her aunt's bony finger jabbing at her, Ah Wong sailing the *Junko* away, her mother's kimono going up in flames. Her heart began to race.

"We will face her in court and we will win," said Jamuka.

"I want to stay here," said Nat, reaching out to stroke Jebe's head.

"You could, but your destiny lies elsewhere. I promised your parents…"

She leaned over, putting her face close to Jebe's. He cocked his face to one side and looked at her with his golden eyes. "But they're dead."

"But their legacy and hopes for your future must be respected."

Jebe licked her cheek. "What hopes? That I study hard, inherit a fortune and have to run a computer games company? What if I don't want to? What if I just want to stay here and be a part of the Clan?"

He looked at her, his eyes softening.

"You are from a very different world to this, Bao Bao. We will come back and visit, but your true path lies in Hong Kong."

"No!"

He put his hand over hers.

"You are as brave as a lion. What you have done to save the Clan and the wolf pack makes me so proud. I am truly honoured that I am your guardian, and as your guardian I must ask that you trust me and honour your parents' wishes."

She let out a deep sigh.

"Can Jebe come with us?" She stroked his head.

CRIMSON POISON

"Jebe must stay here to ensure the survival of the pack."

Nat threw her arms around Jebe's neck, inhaling his scent of warm fur, woodsmoke and pine. She stamped it into her memory, willing herself never to forget.

"I'll be back," she whispered to the wolf.

Chapter Seventy-Five
COMMUNICATION

The buzz from Jamuka's FastPad woke Nat up. She pushed herself up from where she'd been lying across the seat. She was in Fred's old spot in the Overrider. There was so much more room than she'd had in the back, and it was far less bumpy.

She rubbed the sleep from her eyes. Outside it was dark, the full beam of the headlights showed them driving across the flat white expanse of the Steppe.

"It's Wen," said Jamuka, passing over the FastPad.

"*Hai*, you're alive!" said Wen, her face filling the screen.

Nat blinked, her mind going into a spin as her old life collided with the present.

"I've read Jamuka's message. Wow, what an adventure you've had," said Wen, peering closely into camera. "You are one *gun fu* jade babe!"

Nat smiled.

"Did he tell you everything?"

"Yes, all about the ex-Clan guy who was trying

to poison the Clan with Growemup to get back at them."

Nat felt Jamuka tap her on the knee. She looked up from the screen to see him holding a finger to his lips. It suddenly hit her that she was never going to be able to tell the truth about what really happened – the Barzurkans, the Tumen Vachir, Genghis Khan. Secrets were secrets.

"Yes, he was as mad as a box of snakes," she said.

"Must have been. Anyway, you must be as swift as a rocket getting back here. There's been a lot going down and you've missed all the news about an amazing hoax by the Barzurkan army about some super-weapon that even had Mum and Dad fooled!"

Chapter Seventy-Six
CONFRONTATION

"*Zoinks!* We've only got fifteen minutes," said Nat, checking her watch. "We're never going to make it."

They had landed in Chek Lap Kok airport but still had to get across the water to the Hong Kong court building where Wen had said Aunt Vera and Uncle Fergal would be waiting to get the guardian papers stamped. She looked over at Jamuka, who was calmly speaking to an airport official.

"This way," he said, heading towards a doorway.

Nat ran after him, through the door, into a stairwell. They bounded up the steps, taking two at a time, until they came out on to the airport roof. A Speedcopter sat waiting for them, its blades rotating, ready for immediate take-off.

"*Zoula!*" she said, jumping inside.

The door closed, they lifted up into the sky and took off towards Hong Kong. Nat looked down at the flickering skyline. Home at last.

Minutes later they touched down on the top of the

District Court building. Nat climbed out to find Wen and Henry waiting. They ran to meet her, wrapping her up in a tight hug.

"*Ai yah*. You look and smell like a proper explorer," said Wen, letting go.

Nat laughed and looked down at her baggy trousers, black boots and wool sweater. "Not quite Shan-xi, is it?" she said.

"Hurry," said Jamuka. "Lead the way, Henry."

Henry bounded towards the open door. The others followed, clattering down twenty flights of stairs.

"How much further?" shouted Nat.

"One more floor," said Wen, taking two steps at a time.

They flew through a door, coming out into a long corridor. Wigged barristers powered along, cloaks flapping like bats. Wen took the lead, weaving through their midst with Nat, Henry and Jamuka in her wake.

She finally came to a stop outside a large pair of mahogany doors marked "Courtroom Seven". A computer screen above flashed "Court in Session – Walker vs Walker".

"Allow me," said Jamuka, flinging open the doors.

The judge looked up in surprise. On one side of the

court sat Aunt Vera, Uncle Fergal, Prissy and a purse-lipped, grey-haired woman. Nat guessed it had to be the new nanny, Mrs McTavish. They turned, their jaws dropping open.

"Surprise!" said Wen.

Aunt Vera's eyes shot from Wen in her immaculate designer lime-green catsuit to rest on Nat. She looked her up and down from head to toe, taking in the Mongolian tribal clothes, tangled mass of red hair and rosy-cheeked face. Then her gaze fell on Jamuka, who was similarly attired. The sound of a strangled cat erupted from Aunt Vera.

"You went to Mongolia? You defied and lied to me!" she screamed at Nat. She swayed, gripping hold of Uncle Fergal's arm for support. Prissy scowled. Uncle Fergal flushed crimson with embarrassment.

"Let us take our seats," said Jamuka, waving towards a small man wearing a smart grey suit who was busy mopping the sweat from his brow with a canary-yellow silk handkerchief. Nat recognised him. It was Jamuka's lawyer, Mr Chun.

"Henry Walker, get over here right now!" screeched Aunt Vera.

Henry ignored her and carried on walking towards Mr Chun.

"I said now!"

The judge banged her gavel on the desk. "Silence in court! Now. Who do we have here?" she asked, peering over her half-moon glasses.

Jamuka took hold of Nat's hand and led her up to the judge's desk. Out of the corner of her eye she could see Prissy staring daggers at her.

"This is Nat Walker and I am Jamuka, her guardian."

He handed the judge their passports. She thumbed through them and then looked up, peering closely at their Mongolian clothing.

"You look as if you have just arrived from an expedition."

"We have. Our flight just arrived from Mongolia."

Nat smiled and squeezed Jamuka's hand.

"You are a liar!" screeched Aunt Vera from the side of the courtroom. "Nat told me she was staying with Doctor Tang."

"Silence in court!" The judge banged her gavel on the desk again.

She looked down at the papers in front of her and then at each of the lawyers. "I will see you two in my chambers, right now! The rest of you are to remain here. No one is to leave the courtroom, have you got that, Sergeant Yao?"

"Yes, ma'am," said the policeman at the back of the court.

The judge stood up and disappeared through a side door with the two lawyers trotting along in her wake. The door closed. For a moment there was complete silence.

"You've no hope of keeping her," said Aunt Vera, pointing a long bony finger at Jamuka.

"Mrs Walker, I am Nat's legal guardian and you would do well to respect her parents' wishes – and the law," said Jamuka.

"You are a vile, greedy, wicked witch!" said Nat, unable to swallow her feelings.

Prissy glared. "Don't you say that about my mum, you—"

"Stop this ruckus or you will all be in contempt of court!" Sergeant Yao came running to the front. "There will be silence now until the judge is back," he ordered.

Nat went and sat down next to Henry. He squeezed her hand.

"I hate Mummy," he whispered.

Nat didn't dare look up at the wall of vile Walkers opposite.

"Me too."

"Shhhhh!" said Jamuka.

They sat in silence, Sergeant Yao keeping guard in the middle of the courtroom. Nat was wondering just how long they were going to be kept in such heated suspense when the judge re-entered the courtroom with the two lawyers. She resumed her position and turned to Aunt Vera.

"Jamuka Borjigin is Nat's legal guardian. They were away on holiday. And yet you filled in a claim of abandonment to request sole guardianship? Is this correct, Mrs Walker?"

"It's not like that—" said Aunt Vera.

"You have wasted my time and this court's time, and have attempted to make a mockery of our child-protection laws. You are liable for all fees pertaining to this case, you are forbidden access to the Walker Trust and must repay everything you have spent from it. I am also imposing a fine of ten thousand dollars. Case dismissed!"

She slammed down her gavel, stood up from her chair and once again swept out of the side door.

Aunt Vera fainted. Henry and Wen let out a loud cheer. Nat threw her arms around Jamuka and he hugged her tight.

"Let's go home," he said.

Chapter Seventy-Seven
"SURPRISE"

Nat walked up the gangway on to the deck of the *Junko*. The sun was shining from a clear sky. A light breeze, carrying warm air, blew across the blue waters of Victoria Harbour. She was home at last.

"Welcome, Miss Walker," said a tall woman in a white uniform. She had her head bowed low, her long dark hair tied back at the nape of her neck. When she looked up she was smiling.

"You must be Ah Ping," said Nat, holding out her hand.

Ah Ping nodded.

"Your new housekeeper, or perhaps I should say boatkeeper."

Nat laughed. "Yes, boatkeeper. How was your journey?"

"My trip from the New Territories was swift. With all the computers on board the *Junko* is easy to sail."

Frantic chirping broke out on the upper deck. Nat looked over to see Jamuka holding up Gobi's cage. He sang back to her; she chirped even more loudly.

"This arrived for you a few moments ago."

Ah Ping held out a small red box. A label on the front read "Natalie Walker, the *Junko. Handle with extreme care*".

Nat's hand trembled.

"Thanks. I'll take it to my cabin."

She closed the door and sat down on her bunk. The last time she'd seen Fizz he lay broken inside a wooden box. And it was all her fault.

She took a deep breath and opened the lid, dreading what she might find. The box was lined with black velvet. Inside lay Fizz, his eyes closed. His emerald scales had been polished to glittering perfection. His snout glowed warm amber.

She gently lifted him out of the box. His bright-green eyes snapped open. His wings unfurled, the broken one now perfectly repaired.

"Hello, Nat. It's good to see you again. How are you?" he said, cocking his head to one side.

"Fizz?" she said in surprise.

"Yes, do you like my new voice? Big upgrade. Higher-resolution two-inch screen and a custom-designed CRU processor..."

Nat grinned. *"Zoinks!* This is so *ku*. I've missed

you so much."

"*By my calculations I have been asleep for twelve days.*"

"Asleep?" Nat wasn't sure about that. "I'm sorry, it was my fault. I had to use your wing to cut a rope…"

"*Do not apologise. I'm glad to be of service.*"

Nat's bedroom door burst open. Henry came rushing in, followed by Wen.

"Daddy dropped me off at the quay. I can stay for the whole month," he said, jumping on to the bed. "Nasty Nanny McTavish got her marching orders. Mummy's gone to a sanatorium for her mental health and Prissy is working at Shan-xi stocking shelves for the rest of the summer to pay off her fashion bill. So I get to stay with you."

"And as of one hour ago I am officially forgiven by my parents for deceiving them and flying off to Borneo without their permission. My mother saved me by saying she thinks I have the makings of a top scientist. Or spy," said Wen.

"*Ku!*" said Nat, hugging her two best friends.

There was a tap on the door. Jamuka walked in.

"Tea is served," he said with a short bow.

"*Let's go,*" said Fizz, flying up into the air and on to Nat's shoulder.

CRIMSON POISON

Everyone just stopped and stared, their jaws hanging open. Nat put her hand to her shoulder. Fizz was perched up there like a real-life parrot.

"Now, that is seriously *ding*," said Wen.

"Hey, can NutNut get an upgrade too?" said Henry. "I've always wanted the eighth-generation model."

"Your father's plan is coming true," said Jamuka.

"What plan?" said Nat.

"Your father designed Fizz to be a sentient robot. He wanted to make him as much like a living creature as possible. But he was limited by the technology of the time."

"*I think, I speak, I fly. I have work to do on the feeling part though.*"

Jamuka moved to the doorway. "Ah Ping's tea awaits. If you'll please follow me."

"What happened to Ah Wong?" said Henry.

"Jamuka sent Mr Chun, the lawyer, up to Dazhou. He's terminating her employment and giving her a lifetime ban on ever contacting us ever again."

"Maybe we could do that with Mummy too?"

Nat put her arm around her cousin's shoulders.

"Let's head up on deck. I can smell cherry cakes."

With Fizz on her shoulder and her two best friends at her side Nat climbed out on to the deck of the

Junko. The sails were raised and ballooning with wind, ready to carry them out of Victoria Harbour for their sunset sail.

"We're home at last," Nat whispered to Fizz.

"For the moment. Though I'm looking forward to our move to London."

Nat frowned. "London?"